Text copyright © 2011 Zetta Elliott
All rights reserved
Printed in the United States of America

The poem in chapter 13, "In Flanders Fields," was written in 1915 by John McCrae.

Published by AmazonEncore
P.O. Box 400818
Las Vegas, NV 89140

ISBN-13: 9781612182681
ISBN-10: 1612182682

ZETTA ELLIOTT

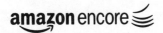

For Kodie.

PREFACE

I live in Brooklyn, and I believe in magic.

For years I passed a large boulder in Prospect Park that marked the site of Battle Pass. The plaque on it explained that American and German soldiers had fought there at the start of the Revolutionary War. Sometimes when I walked by the boulder I would wonder, "What if that plaque was really a door that opened late at night?" In my mind's eye I could see dimly lit stairs leading down into the earth—but I couldn't see farther than that.

On the first warm day of spring in 2010, I walked up Flatbush Avenue toward Grand Army Plaza. Through the cast iron fence on my left, I heard a rustling in the dry brown leaves that covered the ground. I assumed it was just a squirrel and so continued on my way. The rustling persisted, however, and so I stopped—and the rustling stopped. I resumed walking, and whatever small creature was following me continued as well. I stopped—it stopped. I walked on and it pursued me. I finally turned and searched the park floor but couldn't find a chipmunk or squirrel or any other source of the sound. What I did see (in my mind's eye) were three kids—two boys and a girl. I saw something invisible grab the youngest boy and drag him along the ground. His friends came to his aid and saved him from being dragged underground. I stored that scene in the back of my mind and walked on.

During the summer I came across an online article about an eighteenth-century ship that was found during construction at Ground Zero. "Why would a boat be buried underground?" I wondered. Archaeologists suggested it had simply been used as landfill when lower Manhattan was being expanded in the seventeen hundreds. I had other ideas but tucked them away until November. That's when I found a beautiful cowrie shell on the ground near my home. I assumed it had fallen off someone's jewelry or bag and simply put it in my pocket and walked on. A week later my favorite literacy organization, Behind the Book, brought me to JHS 13 in East Harlem. Though they were studying *Bird*, Ms. Mayers's sixth-grade students asked me to tell them about my latest story, and so I told them about the rustling leaves, the voices I kept hearing, and the scenes unfolding in my mind. They urged me to finish the story and return to tell them how it ended. I promised that I would.

In December, I found a second cowrie shell—tiny, white, fragile, yet miraculously intact. Two perfect shells— once used as currency in Africa—lying on the streets of Brooklyn, waiting for me to pick them up. It *had* to be a sign. For years I had wanted to write about the African Burial Ground in lower Manhattan—a sacred site outside the city limits where, up until 1794, fifteen thousand free and enslaved blacks were buried. Four hundred and nineteen of those burials were uncovered in 1991 during construction of the Ted Weiss Federal Building. Community members mobilized and fought for the study and preservation of the remains, and today an impressive monument marks the resting place of those unnamed souls who built the colony that became New York City.

A week before Christmas, I sat down and began writing *Ship of Souls*. For me, Christmas is a magical season filled with miraculous stories. I knew that my story would be about redemption and release. By the lights that decorated my little tree, I wrote through the blizzard that immobilized the city. I told a story of loss and loyalty, an urban fantasy woven together with fragments of the city's history and my own contemporary reality.

I've always known there was magic in this city. Or rather, I *believed* that magic was possible here, and so magical things have happened to me. I didn't feel that way when I was growing up in Canada. I dedicate this book to my cousin Kodie, who lives in Canada and so may have to dream himself into existence just as I did when I was his age.

1.

"Walk like a man, not like a pimp." That's what my mother used to say. She was my best friend. That might sound weird, but my mom was all I ever had. No dad, no aunts and uncles or cousins. Mom didn't like to talk about our family, but I knew it wasn't normal, the way we lived. I used to tell myself that Mom must have testified against the mafia and so the FBI put us in their witness protection program. Somewhere out there was a whole other life filled with people who loved us but couldn't be trusted with our new identities. That's better than the other possibility, which is that my father's some kind of psycho stalker. Or maybe he just couldn't bother to stick around. Whenever I asked about him, Mom would say, "Don't I love you enough?" And I wouldn't ask any more questions after that because she did. My mother was all I needed.

One time when I was eight, I had a really bad cold and couldn't sleep. The light was on in the hallway, so I just left my bedroom door open a crack and got down on the floor with my pillow and my book. I must have fallen asleep after a while because I didn't hear the intercom or the doorbell. But I woke up when I heard someone at the front door—someone my mom knew but didn't want to let in.

"He's mine."

"He's *not* yours—he's *ours*."

"You promised, Neil. You promised you'd stay away."

"And I've kept my end of the deal. You know I have. I just want to see him."

"He's sleeping."

"So let me watch my boy sleep. Five minutes, Irene. Five minutes with my boy."

For a moment Mom said nothing. I stared at her hand gripping the doorknob and willed her other hand to slide the chain off and let my dad inside. It was him—I just knew it was him.

"I can't. I'm sorry, Neil. I just can't."

"But why—"

"You *know* why!" she hissed at him. "You know damn well why we have to live this way. You made your choice."

"And you made yours, Irene. Why can't the boy make up his own mind? He's old enough now."

"No. He's my child and I'll do whatever it takes to keep him safe."

"And what if something happens to you, Irene? Then what?"

"Nothing's going to happen to me."

"How do you know? You can't predict the future."

"Predict? No. But I *can* plan." Mom shook her head. "You're not part of the plan, Neil."

The man pulled back from the door. "Time will tell," I heard him say, and then Mom closed and locked the door.

When I asked her about it the next day, Mom gave me a real funny look. Then she pressed her palm against my forehead and said the fever must have given me a crazy dream. Later, when cancer made a liar of my mom (*nothing's going to happen to me*), I thought maybe the man at the door would come back for me—give me that chance to make up my own mind. But he didn't. Maybe it was just a dream after all.

She was tight-lipped about my father, but when it came to other stuff, I could talk to my mom about pretty much anything. Sometimes I worried that I wasn't "black enough." I'm not a total geek or anything, but I'd been home-schooled for most of my life, and that meant I didn't spend a lot of time with other kids. When Mom got sick, I had to enroll in a public school, and I didn't exactly fit in. Kids on my block called me "reject." Grown folks at church called me "an old soul." One girl at school told me I talked like a white boy. But when I ask Mom about it, she just said, "You *are* black. And nothing you say or do or pretend to be will ever change that fact. So just be yourself, Dmitri. *Be who you are.*"

I still hear her voice every day, and sometimes I even talk back. Mostly I just try to do the things I know she'd want me to do. Like keep my grades up, respect my elders, speak proper English—stuff like that.

One of the nurses at the hospital gave me a pink ribbon pin to put on my jacket, but I put it in my pocket instead. I didn't want to be a walking advertisement for cancer. Plus, you get a ribbon when you win some kind of contest, and this time, I didn't win. I lost. Cancer won.

Sometimes I push the pin into my finger just to make sure I don't forget what losing feels like. I prick my skin and squeeze out a little blood. Feeling pain means I'm still alive, and I know Mom would want me to keep on living. Problem is, most days I just feel numb. When I'm not numb, I'm miserable. And even when I'm not miserable, I'm still alone.

2.

Right after Christmas a blizzard hit the city. This lady on our block went into labor, but the streets weren't plowed, so she couldn't get to the hospital. She tried walking through all that snow but only made it as far as our building. She had the baby right there in the lobby with the help of some of our neighbors. They called an ambulance, but it never came and the baby died. All because of a blizzard. I never told my mom. She was upstairs "dying with dignity." At least that's what Marva and the hospice lady said. To me, it looked like Mom was just too tired and weak to wake up.

Marva was my mother's best friend—her only friend, really. We mostly kept to ourselves, but Marva lived on our floor, and she was there with us at the end. When Mom passed and the hospice lady went away, Marva let me come stay with her. But ACS sent a social worker to check on me, and she said I had to go with her. Marva worked nights as a security guard, and that meant I was sleeping alone in the apartment. Marva said, "Don't worry, baby, I got it all under control." But Marva never came for me.

Now I'm in the system, and I don't really know what's going to happen next. Jimmy, this kid in the bunk above mine, acts like he's an expert on foster care. Mom used to tell me to make small talk when I wanted to get to know someone new. I get kind of nervous around people I don't know. Not Jimmy—he just dives right in.

"You a new kid, or did you get sent back?"

"Sent back?"

"Sure—happens all the time," he says. "Foster parents change their mind, or you screw up and lose your shine, and next thing you know you're right back where you started."

"This isn't where I started," I say with just a hint of attitude.

"So you're a new kid."

"Yeah, I guess."

"Welcome to purgatory, otherwise known as 'limbo-land.' This is where we wait to get pulled up to heaven or dragged down into hell."

I don't know what this crazy kid is talking about, so I just take a book out of my bag and pretend to be absorbed. Jimmy hangs over the edge of the bed watching me until I think blood's going to start pouring out of his ears. Finally he jumps down and sits on the edge of my bed. "What you reading?"

Before I can answer, Jimmy rips the book out of my hands and looks at the picture on the cover. "Looks lame."

"Hand it over, then."

He flings the book at me and uses his heel to kick my suitcase, which is shoved under the bed. "You got a lock on this?"

I hesitate and wonder if I should lie. Telling the truth might just encourage him to snoop around. But something tells me this kid's a pro when it comes to lying, so I settle for telling the truth. "No. Why?"

"Stuff gets snatched all the time around here. Caseworkers think they got us locked down with all their rules and regulations, but they don't know half the stuff that goes down around here—especially after dark. Soon as they call lights out, all the heavyweights go to work—stealing, dealing. How old are you?"

"Eleven."

Jimmy nods like that's a good thing. "You got a year before they put you in the juvie joint."

"Juvie joint? What's that?"

"That's where they put the kids who got records. You know—junior criminals."

My heart's starting to speed up, but I keep my nose buried in my book so Jimmy won't see the fear in my eyes. I'm hoping that if I show no interest, Jimmy will take a hint and climb up into his own bunk. But Jimmy's not even looking at me. His eyes are fixed on the window even though there's nothing to see through the frosted glass.

"Yeah—group home's no joke. I had a cousin who wound up in a group home. They messed him up pretty bad. Between the gangs and the pervs, Alfie didn't stand a chance. The way he tells it, group home's just like training camp for prison—a whole bunch of bad asses trying to prove who's on top." Jimmy smirks at me. "All I'm saying is, don't drop the soap!" He laughs at the terror in my eyes before pulling himself back up to the top bunk.

I lie in my own bed and will myself not to cry. *Cheese and rice.* Mom told me never to take the Lord's name in vain, so even though I really need God's help right now, I can't bring myself to say his son's name. So instead I say, *Cheese and rice! Please don't let me get put in a group home. Please.*

The next morning after breakfast, I get called into the caseworker's office. There's an old white lady sitting in the chair beside her desk, so I stand by the door. I look like a soldier standing at ease, but really I've got my fingers crossed behind my back. *Come on, lady*, I plead silently, *take me home. I promise to be the perfect son you've always wanted.*

The caseworker stands and comes around her desk to put a hand on my shoulder. "D, this is Mrs. Martin. I've just been telling her a bit about you."

I extend my hand and say, "Pleased to meet you, Mrs. Martin."

The old lady's face lights up, and I know she's impressed by my good manners. I never imagined a white person would want to adopt me, but Mom used to say beggars can't be choosers. I decide then and there that I *will* beg this woman to take me home if I have to.

"It's a pleasure to meet you, D," she says. "And I'd just like to offer you my sincere condolences on the passing of your mother."

I wasn't ready for that. I never did figure out the best way to handle other folks' sympathy. I drop my eyes and say, "Thank you, ma'am."

Mrs. Martin looks at the caseworker and says, "Poor thing. So young to have lost so much."

The caseworker gives my shoulder a squeeze and says, "Why don't I go get another chair so you two can spend some time getting to know one another?"

"That would be lovely," says Mrs. Martin.

I smile and nod eagerly like there's nothing I'd rather do than chat up this old lady. How long do I get to sell myself? Every Wednesday the weather woman on channel four features a kid who's up for adoption. I always felt sorry for those kids, but now the shoe's on the other foot. Should I pull out all the stops and try to dazzle her with my brilliance? Or should I stick with being humble and polite? I decide to start with some flattery.

"I like your hat," I say with a fake look of admiration.

Mrs. Martin reaches up a hand to proudly stroke the tacky flowers spilling over the brim. "Thank you, D. It's not my best—I save that one for Sunday. Was your mother active in the church?"

Active? Mom and I sat in the same pew every week, but that sounds passive, not active. "She taught Sunday school for a few years," I say. I decide not to tell Mrs. Martin about the Christian Singles Group. Mom always said it should have been called the Christian Spinsters Group since there were ten women for every man. She went to a few meetings and then quit. "We went to the AME church near our building," I add.

"Well, I'm Unitarian and I live in a house. Have you ever lived in a house before, D?"

"No, ma'am."

"I think you'll like it. There's a yard out back and you'll have your own room. I have a tenant on the top floor, but he works nights and mostly keeps to himself."

Mrs. Martin's using the future tense—does that mean she's already decided to take me home? Just then the caseworker returns with an extra chair. I thank her, sit down, and wait to see what happens next.

"I was just telling D about my house," Mrs. Martin says. "It's much too large for a little old lady like me. I had hoped to foster a girl this time, but I think you're right, Ms. Ward. D's a sweet boy."

Ms. Ward turns to me. "Mrs. Martin lives near a magnet school, D, so you'll be able to continue with your studies." To the old lady she says, "D's an excellent student—he's won a number of prizes for academic achievement."

"Your mother must have been very proud of you," Mrs. Martin says.

"Yes, ma'am. She was," I say.

When the caseworker realizes I have nothing else to say, she speaks on my behalf. "D's never been in any kind of trouble, and you can see how respectful he is."

"Yes," says Mrs. Martin, "I can tell already he won't be anything like the others."

The caseworker sees my confusion and rushes to explain. "Mrs. Martin had a bad experience last year with a couple of brothers she agreed to foster."

The tacky flowers dance a bit as Mrs. Martin shakes her head. "It was dreadful! I hated to send them back, but those two boys would have tried the patience of a saint. They ate as much as grown men and helped themselves to anything that wasn't nailed down…"

"Well, I can assure you that you won't have any trouble with D. Right?"

Ms. Ward looks at me. This is my cue, my last chance to seal the deal. What should I say?

"I—I don't eat much. And I can help out around the house—I'm used to doing chores. And, well…" I search for something else to say but feel my throat closing as tears fill my eyes. All I manage to squeeze out is, "I really need a home."

Mrs. Martin blinks her eyes, then reaches into her pocketbook to get a tissue. She hands one to me and uses another to dab at her eyes. "Bless you, child. I know God has a plan for us." To Ms. Ward she says, "Can I take him home now?"

"Well, you're already in the system, so I should be able to expedite this paperwork. What do you think, D? Are you ready to go?"

And that's how I came to live with Mrs. Martin. Things were pretty good at first. I never had a grandmother before, but Mrs. Martin was just how I imagined a grandma to be. She cooked my favorite meals, baked cookies for me to have when I got home from school, and she even gave me an allowance! In exchange all I had to do was act grateful, and that wasn't hard because I *was* grateful. Sometimes I'd think about Jimmy and wonder if he was still waiting for another foster home. There was no way I was going to give Mrs. Martin any reason to send me back. I wasn't just good—I was better than good. I became Perfect-me, the best possible version of my true self.

Then one day Ms. Ward came to visit us, and she mentioned a newborn baby who'd been abandoned by her crack addict mother. Mrs. Martin had been wanting to foster a little girl, so I guess she thought this was her chance. Ms. Ward came back the next day with a tiny little baby who makes a whole lot of noise. Her name's Mercy, and it's not really her fault. She was born addicted to the same stuff her mother was on. She's going though withdrawal, and that means she needs a lot of time and attention. Not even

Perfect-me can compete with a sad little crack baby, so I just plug my ears and try to help out with all the household stuff that Mrs. Martin no longer has time to do.

I don't mind going to the store on my own. Truth is, I prefer it. Somehow Mrs. Martin never heard of "white flight." When all her white friends left because black people started moving into the neighborhood, Mrs. Martin just stayed put. Now *she's* the minority, but it doesn't seem to bother her. Where I live now is a lot like where I used to live before, except people sometimes look at me funny when I go out with Mrs. Martin. Everyone knows a black boy like me doesn't belong with an old white lady like her. But it wasn't like there was a line of black folks waiting outside of Children's Services. None of them came forward when I needed a home, so I don't need their fake concern now.

3.

My new school is about the same as my old school. Ms. Ward, my caseworker, made sure the principal knew I was a "special case," and so all my teachers treat me that way. They know I'm a foster kid, but I don't have to be Perfect-me at school. Just being quiet and smart's enough.

To the other kids, I'm no one worth noticing. I didn't have a lot of friends at my old school since I was only there a couple of months, and I probably won't have many friends here, either. I joined the math club because the coach invited me, and it'd be rude to say, "I'd rather be alone." I like numbers because they're constant. Predictable. Some numbers even go on into infinity. Numbers aren't like people.

On Monday during math club, a tall black man wearing a kufi comes into our room. He has a winter coat on, but it's unzipped so I can see the gold embroidery on the front of his long blue shirt. Mr. Powell goes over to talk to the man, and after a few moments he turns and points to me. Then he says, "D, could you come over here for a minute?"

As always, I do as I'm told. "Yes, Mr. Powell?"

"D, this is Mr. Diallo. He's looking for someone to tutor his son in math. The job pays ten dollars an hour. You interested?"

"Sure," I say, nice and calm like I make that kind of money all the time. "When do I start?"

"As soon as possible," says Mr. Diallo. "I brought my son—he's waiting outside."

All three of us go out into the hallway. A tall kid in a red hoodie is leaning against the lockers. His back is to us, and that seems to anger Mr. Diallo.

"Hakeem!"

The kid throws a sullen look over his shoulder but says nothing. The hood partly hides his face, but I know this kid. He's a star athlete who just happens to be two grades ahead of me. He's in the regular middle school that shares the building with my magnet school.

"I am talking to you, Hakeem. Show respect!" Mr. Diallo's voice booms down the empty hallway. "And take off that hood—you look like a criminal."

Keem Diallo rolls over so that his back is pressed against the lockers. He pulls the hood off his head, and I see he's wearing a kufi, too. I've seen Keem around school, and he never had a kufi on then. Keem sweeps his eyes over me but doesn't say a word.

Mr. Diallo turns his attention back to me. "My son has basketball practice every day until four p.m. On Tuesdays and Thursdays he will go straight from practice to the library. You can tutor him there."

"Yes, sir," I say. Then I turn to Keem and hold out my hand. "I'm D." I hope he just gives me a regular handshake and not some five-step homeboy greeting.

Keem just stares at me for a moment, but before his father can yell at him again, he pulls his hand out of the hoodie's front pocket and shakes my hand—once. "Keem."

"So…what sort of math problems are you having trouble with?" I ask.

Mr. Diallo throws up his hands. "Everything! He needs help with everything!"

Keem sulks but dares not look his father in the eye. "I said I'd do better."

"How can you do better when you don't even know what to do?" Mr. Diallo turns to Mr. Powell. "With my two jobs, I simply don't have time to tutor him myself. I thank you for your assistance with this matter."

"I'm happy to help. And your son's in good hands—D's the brightest student I've ever had the honor to teach."

That puts a wide grin on my face until I catch a glimpse of Keem—he's looking at me like I'm something he just scraped off the bottom of his size-twelve shoe. Mr. Diallo puts his hand on my shoulder and says, "You bring honor to your family, young man." That wipes off what's left of my smile. There's no one left to be proud of me.

Keem pulls the hood of his sweatshirt back over his head and follows his father down the hall. Mr. Powell and I go back into the classroom. I bury myself in the college-level algebra problem that's scribbled on the board.

4.

On Tuesday I stand in front of the library and wait for Keem to show up for his first math lesson. He's a few minutes late, but I decide to let it slide. I want to say, "My time's valuable, you know." But what else do I have to do? Besides, there's this girl—Nyla—who hangs out with the kamikaze skater kids who flip their boards off the library's front steps. She watches them and I watch her. When Keem finally shows up, I see him watching her, too. He's slick, though. Keem knows how to watch a girl and not get caught. Maybe he's got something to teach me after all.

We go inside and find a table in a corner of the youth wing that's not too rowdy. I've already decided on a few topics of conversation and so jump right in. "You know, 'algebra' comes from the Arabic word *Al-Jabr*. In the Middle Ages, Muslims introduced Europeans to a lot of important mathematical concepts."

Keem looks at me like I'm nuts. "I didn't come here for a history lesson. You're supposed to help me with math."

Small talk is tough.

"I know," I say, "but math *has* history." I seriously doubt Keem and I have anything else in common, so I decide to try my next topic: religion. "So…when do you pray?" I ask.

"What?"

I fight the urge to duck. Keem looks pissed, so I follow up with a quick explanation for my question. "It's just that—well, I thought Muslims had to pray five times a day. You can't really do that when you're at school, right?"

Keem just stares at me for a moment. Then he says, "*Qadaa.* I make it up later when I'm at home."

I nod and think about saying, "That's cool," but decide to just keep my mouth shut.

"We should probably get started," Keem says in a neutral voice. He opens his binder and takes out his most recent test. "If I don't boost my grades, Coach'll have to bench me."

The first thing I see is the big red D at the top of the page. I'm no miracle worker, and I don't want to make any promises I can't keep. Besides, I always thought the rules were bent for star athletes. "They say you'll probably get drafted before you graduate."

For some reason, Keem doesn't take this as a compliment. "I'm *going* to college. And I'm going to *graduate* from college."

"Yeah?"

"Yeah."

I want to say, "What if some team offers you ten million dollars to play for them?" But I decide to play it safe instead. "I guess it's good to have a backup plan in case you get injured or something."

Keem nods, then surprises me by saying, "People think basketball's my world, but…I got other skills."

"Yeah? Like what?"

Keem fidgets a bit and looks around before answering. "I cook."

"Food?" I ask like a moron.

"What else?" Keem replies. "My dad—he's from Senegal. But my mom—she's Bangladeshi. So in our house there are lots of different spices and different ways of preparing food."

"Fusion."

"What?" Keem glares at me like I've just said "phooey."

"Fusion," I explain. "That's what they call food that blends different traditions." Mom used to take me to this Ethiopian-Cuban place in the city. That was the best food I ever had! But I don't want to think about my mother right now. I don't need to start blubbering in front of this jock.

"Oh, I get it." Keem relaxes and starts doodling on a blank page in his notebook. "Well, I figure if ballin' doesn't work out, I could always open my own restaurant and serve all different kinds of food—maybe soul food but with an African or Asian twist. And no swine."

"You're making me hungry," I say with a grin. Keem almost laughs, and we turn our attention back to his test.

To my surprise, it isn't as bad as I thought it would be. "Half of these answers are almost right, you know."

Keem frowns. "You don't get points for being 'almost' right."

"I know. But see this problem? You got ninety percent of it right. It's just the last step you messed up. I can teach you that in, like, five minutes. If you'd solved these four problems, your grade would have been a B instead of a D."

Keem stares at the red X marks on his test. "For real?"

This is my moment to shine. "For real. Here—let me show you a little trick I learned in math club."

When our hour is up, Keem shoves his books into his bag and slaps a ten-dollar bill on the table. "Thanks," he says before getting up and heaving the bag onto his back. "See you on Thursday?"

"Sure," I say. Keem nods, tucks his basketball under his arm, and walks out of the library without saying another word. I pick up the money and stare at it for a moment. Mom would want me to put it in the bank, but right now I'm thinking about getting a couple slices and a can of soda. Without Mom around, there's probably not much chance of me going to college, anyway.

I leave the library and head straight for the pizza joint. In my head I'm doing the math: twenty bucks a week times however long it takes to get Keem's grades up. Three weeks? Ten? Maybe the rest of the school year?

By the time my slices come out of the oven, I've already figured out how to spend the money I'll make as a tutor. I'm so into my dreams and schemes that I don't see this jerk Selwyn standing outside. Selwyn's in the sixth grade, too, but he isn't supposed to be. Mom always told me to watch out for kids who got left back. Most of them are all right, she said, but sometimes they turn into crabs in a barrel, willing to drag down anyone who's on his way up. Selwyn's that kind of kid.

"Hey, look who it is—the brainiac. You smart enough to get the special?"

"Yeah," I say warily.

"Good—that's one slice for me and one for my boy." Selwyn grabs the paper bag holding my food. I don't let go at first, but I've got five dollars left in my pocket and don't plan to get my butt kicked by two kids over some pizza.

Selwyn tugs the bag a bit harder and I let go. "Thanks, geek," he says with an ugly sneer.

"Hey!"

All of us turn and see Keem coming out of a nearby bodega with a brown-bagged drink. He casually twists the cap off the bottle and tosses it into a wire trash bin on the corner. "Where you going with my food? D—didn't I tell you to get me two slices?"

It takes me a couple of seconds to understand what Keem's doing, but as soon as I figure it out, I slip into my assigned role. "Uh—yeah, Keem. And I did, but…these guys said they're hungry, too." I look at Selwyn and force my lips not to curl up into a smug smile.

"He's with you?" Selwyn asks, amazed.

"Yeah," Keem replies, standing real close so his height is more intimidating. "He's with me."

Selwyn waits for the punch line but then realizes Keem's for real. And with those three words (*he's with me*), I go from being prey to being protected property. I'm untouchable now!

I can't help but smirk a little as Selwyn hands me back my food and shuffles off with his boy, leaving me alone with Keem.

"You all right?" Keem asks in his usual flat tone.

I just nod since I'm not quite able to look Keem in the eye. "Thanks," I mumble and extend the bag holding my pizza. "Want a slice?"

"Nah." Keem takes a swig from his bottle of Gatorade and looks over my head to the opposite side of the street.

As I turn to go, I let my eyes roam along the block. On the other side of the street I see Nyla with one of the skater kids. She's watching us.

"There's your girl," I tell Keem, but then I look at his face and realize he already knows she's there. That's probably why he helped me—to impress a girl. Not because he wants to be my friend.

Keem's trying to act cool, but I can tell he's feeling hectic inside. He doesn't know whether he should keep up the tough-guy routine or try being nice to me. Keem opts for the second option and puts his arm around my shoulder.

"Come on. I'll walk you home." Keem shepherds me down the block like I'm his little brother or something. I glance across the street and see Nyla smiling at me. For some reason I feel bold enough to wave and smile back. For just an instant, Nyla flicks her eyes at Keem. Then she turns and walks off in the opposite direction. Keem waits until we reach the end of the block and turn the corner, then he takes back his arm. He exhales loudly like he'd been holding his breath the whole time. I think he's going to say something about Nyla, but instead his voice turns gruff and Keem says, "You got to learn to stand up for yourself, D."

The anger in my voice surprises me more than Keem. "That's easy for you to say—you look like a model, you're built like a giant, and kids at school worship the ground you walk on!"

"Yeah—when they're not calling me a terrorist behind my back. Think I don't know what they say about me as soon as I step off the court? Or what it means when they sit up in the stands and tell me to 'blow up' the competition? We all got our battles, D. We all got to fight for respect."

Before I can think of anything to say, Keem mutters, "Later," and heads down the block. I sink onto the stoop and eat my cold pizza alone.

5.

Girls don't notice me, but that doesn't mean I don't notice them. And most of the girls I notice may be out of my league, but that doesn't stop me from dreaming. I've always been an overachiever, so why shouldn't I set my sights on an eighth-grade girl?

Nyla's like a beautiful sculpture made of onyx and silver. She wears skintight clothes—mostly black—with strategically placed holes held together by safety pins. And boots—army boots. She came to school one day with a full head of hair; the next day, the sides and back of her head were shaved, leaving a silky horse's mane on top. Nyla flipped it to the side so a curtain of black hair fell over her right eye. Next day the mane was cropped short, spiked, and streaked with red. I can't even count all the piercings Nyla's got. Rings loop up the outside of her ears, and huge black plugs fill her earlobes. She's got both eyebrows pierced, a diamond stud in her nose, and a silver ball that rests under her lower lip. I think her tongue might be pierced, too, but I'm not sure 'cause Nyla's never talked to me.

One day this creep slipped his arm around her waist as she walked down the hall, and Nyla threw him against the lockers and cursed him out: "*Nimm deine dreckigen Hände von mir, du verdammter Scheißkerl!*"

That's right—Nyla cursed him out *in German.* He's lucky she didn't slug him—with all those silver rings on her fingers, she'd have left a serious dent in that pretty-boy's face. Nobody messes with Nyla. She's beautiful, but she's *fierce.*

On Wednesday I come out of the lunch line with my tray of crappy food, and Nyla smiles at me. That's right—at *me.* I smile back, and then Nyla nods at the empty stretch of bench to her left. To her right is a loud group of misfits, all of whom are acting like they belong in the same galaxy as Nyla. At first I think it must be a mistake—is Nyla really inviting me to sit next to her, or is she just stretching her neck? I don't want to look like a total reject, but Nyla's eyes are locked on mine and her smile grows wider as I start walking over to her table.

"Hey, D. Grab a seat," she says.

Nyla knows my name? I'm smiling like an idiot, but I can't help myself. I also can't think of anything cool to say. I take a seat next to Nyla and try to look at the other kids she's hanging with. Regine's a track star. Melvin rules at chess. A couple of kids are in the drama club, and the others—combined—have *almost* as many piercings as Nyla. As soon as Nyla opens her mouth, they all quiet down and wait to hear what she's going to say. "Hey, everybody—this is D."

The other kids turn and look at me. Some smile, some nod, some say, "Hey," and one girl with blue extension braids gives me a salute. Then a seventh-grader with the biggest Afro I've ever seen points at me and says, "Hey—I know you."

I shove at least half my corn dog into my mouth so I don't have to say anything. I'm pretty sure that sitting next to Nyla doesn't earn me automatic immunity from insults.

"You're in the math club," he says. When I nod, he goes on. "My sister says you're, like, some kind of kid genius—a total math freak!"

I look down at the carton of milk and bowl of canned pineapple on my tray. Aside from Nyla, these kids aren't exactly what I would call "cool." But they clearly know and like one another—they're friends. Which puts me on the outside. I brace myself for the usual nerd jokes.

Then Nyla slips her arm around my shoulder. "A math freak, huh? Then it's official—you're one of us, D."

I smile at Nyla, but I'm not really sure how to feel. Should I be proud that I belong with a bunch of self-proclaimed freaks? Or should I try to salvage whatever social reputation I have by getting up and sitting some-where else—even if that means eating alone? I finally decide that I'd rather be seen with the wrong kind of kids than be totally invisible.

"So," Nyla says, "what else are you into besides math?"

My mind races as I try to think of something to say that will make me look mature and cool enough to be interesting to an eighth-grade girl. It's hard to focus on anything besides my discovery that Nyla has dimples that only show when she smiles. Finally I settle for a lame but true answer. "I like birds. There are two hundred species in Prospect Park."

I know how lame that sounds, but Nyla just nods and says, "Last of the dinosaurs, right? Maybe I can tag along the next time you go bird-watching."

Before I can tell Nyla that she can tag along ANYTIME, a skinny kid wearing preppy clothes suddenly whispers, "Hottie alert!" and everyone at the table quiets down. I'm so busy looking around for a cute girl that I don't notice Keem's heading over to our table.

"Hey, D. What's up?"

I nearly choke on a chunk of pineapple but manage to cover my mouth before a piece of half-chewed fruit flies out and lands on Keem's new kicks. I feel like I must be dreaming—two of the most popular kids in school talking to me on the same day! "Not much," I stammer nervously. "Just having lunch."

Keem stands there awkwardly. He glances at Nyla, but she's flicking a bottle cap along the tabletop. The girl with the blue braids watches the cap zoom right off the end of the table and yells, "SCORE!"

Keem finally gives up on trying to make Nyla notice him. "See you tomorrow, then. Four o'clock, right?"

"Right. I'll meet you in front of the library," I say.

Keem nods, glances at Nyla one last time, and then walks away. Crushed.

I turn to Nyla and find her watching Keem's back. "Friend of yours?" she asks with her eyes still glued on Keem.

"Tutee," I say before cramming all the remaining pineapple into my mouth. I don't want to talk about Keem.

The kid with the giant Afro says, "Two tea? What's that mean?"

It takes me a few seconds to stop chewing. "I'm tutoring him in math. I'm his tutor, he's my tutee."

Afro-kid nods like he's impressed. "What'd I tell you? The kid's a math genius."

A skinny kid cradling a skateboard says, "Yeah—and look what they make him do: teach the dumb jocks how to count to ten!"

"Keem's not dumb." I'm not sure why I said that, but it's too late to take it back now.

Nyla turns to the skater kid. "What's the Freak's Golden Rule, Jamal?"

He drops his eyes and mumbles, "Don't be a prick." Then he looks at me and says, "Sorry I dissed your friend, D."

I'm about to say, "Keem's not my friend," when a girl with a shaved head and a bolt through her nose says, "My brother plays ball in the park with Keem. He gets mad respect—on and off the court."

The girl with blue braids looks straight at Nyla and says, "He also gets any girl he wants."

Nyla sucks her teeth, but her eyes find Keem sitting with the other jocks on the far side of the cafeteria. "We'll see about that," she says, then gets up and carries her tray over to the trash.

The noise level in the cafeteria seems to drop a notch as Nyla walks down the main aisle and out into the schoolyard. Some of the freaks get up and follow their leader. Others stay and finish the crappy school lunch. A quiet girl with long locks slides along the bench and asks if I can help her with her math homework. I say, "Sure," and think maybe I really do belong here with the rest of these outcasts.

6.

After school I decide to skip the library and head straight to the park. I haven't been on my own much lately, and while I like making new friends, I'm not going to get used to their company. Here today, gone tomorrow. That's what people are like.

Birds are different. Some birds migrate, but there are plenty that stay in the city all year round. I don't have to go to the park to find them—pigeons are everywhere, which is probably why they get kicked around so much. I think pigeons are beautiful—that iridescent ring around their necks looks just like a rainbow. But that's one of those things I've learned to keep to myself. Otherwise kids'll call me a wuss or a punk—or worse. When I'm in the park, there's no one around to tease me for liking birds. They're related to dinosaurs, you know, which makes them really ancient. And raptors—they're some of the fiercest preda-tors around. I saw a hawk tear into a live rabbit once—blood and guts everywhere! Bird-watching's definitely *not* for the faint of heart.

Today I head deep into the park, away from the sports fields and the playgrounds that attract other kids. Spring's coming, and we changed all the clocks last weekend, so the days are getting longer. Only a few patches of dirty snow are left in the park, and all the dog poop people never bothered to scoop shows up now as uneven clumps of thick green grass. If you look closely—and watch where you step—you can see tiny purple shoots poking up here and there, proof that life's stirring underground. My mom used to love crocuses. Purple was her favorite color. Seems like each new season brings fresh reminders that she's gone.

The ravine's a good place to spot birds, and with no leaves on the trees yet, it's easy to find their nests and track their movements. Male birds usually have brighter colors, so the challenge is to find their mates. Mostly I listen for their calls because my eyes aren't great these days. I was supposed to get my eyes checked last fall, but then Mom went into the hospital, and my vision wasn't anyone's priority anymore. I guess I should tell Mrs. Martin because sometimes it's hard for me to see the board at school. But for now I just sit close to the front of the classroom and squint when I can't see clear.

It's dim in the tree-filled ravine, so I take my time heading down the concrete stairs that are built into the steep slope. I'm watching my feet, not the trees, and that's how I notice an injured bird huddled in a pile of dry leaves not far from the steps. It's cooing like a mourning dove, but it's got the wrong coloring. I stand still and try to figure out a way to reach the bird without startling it. As soon as I step on those dry leaves, the bird might panic and try to fly away. I can't see whether its wings are damaged, but that's the only reason a bird like that would be on the ground instead of up in a tree.

"Hey, there. I'm D." I figure a little small talk can't hurt, especially if I use a soothing tone of voice. "Looks like you could use some help. Can I come over there?"

"Yes, please do."

I blink my eyes a couple of times even though it's my ears that are playing tricks on me. I could swear that bird just talked to me! Then again, I hear my mom's voice all the time. Maybe there's just something wrong with me.

I push that thought aside and go on talking to the injured bird. It must be some kind of dove because it's pure white. I've seen white pigeons before, but this bird's smaller. Maybe someone released it at a wedding—people get married in the botanic garden all the time, and that's not far from here.

"OK," I say as I take my first step toward the bird, "I'm coming over there now. Don't mind all the noise—it's just these dry leaves, no need to be alarmed. I'll move real slow, like this. See?"

The dove coos some more, but it doesn't flinch as I move toward it. When I'm about a foot away, I squat down and brush away some of the leaves that are covering its body. Right away the bird starts to tremble, and I realize the dead leaves were keeping it warm. "It's OK," I assure it. "I'm going to take care of you." The bird seems to understand me because it wriggles its body closer to mine and even lets me stroke its body with my hand. I know feathers are supposed to be soft, but this bird's feathers feel like satin! Before I can pet it a second time, the bird makes a small leap, and I catch hold of it with my hands.

Up close, the bird doesn't look white anymore. In a way, it doesn't even look like a bird! In my hands it seems to glow as if lit from within by a white flame. The next instant it cools, hardens, and glitters like a tear-shaped diamond. Then it warms again and settles between my palms like a precious pearl.

"I really need to get my eyes checked," I say to myself.

"Why—do you doubt your senses?" asks the shimmering globe.

"You can talk?"

"I can communicate, yes. You like birds, don't you?"

Before I can answer, the white orbs turns back into a dove. It whimpers softly, which makes me forget all the other questions I was ready to ask. "Are—are you hurt?"

"No, but I am weak." She snuggles close to my down jacket. "And a little cold."

Without any hesitation I unzip my jacket and place the bird inside, next to my heart. "Is that better?"

She coos once more and looks up at me. "It's getting dark."

After several minutes of gazing at the luminous bird, it's hard to tell whether or not the sky's growing dark. When I came to the park, I had planned to stay for at least a couple of hours. Still, I find myself saying, "I guess it's time to go home." And with that, I climb back up the steps that lead out of the ravine.

As I walk back to Mrs. Martin's place, I start to notice that things look different. Clearer. Brighter. And I don't normally look forward to going home, but tonight I can't wait to turn my key in the lock. I walk faster than usual, checking on my precious cargo every few seconds to make sure she's OK.

I go straight up to my room and rearrange the pillows on my bed to make a soft resting place for the bird. Then I take one of Mrs. Martin's good plush towels out of the linen closet and wrap it around my new friend. "Is that OK?" I ask her. "Are you warm enough?"

"Yes, thank you. You're the perfect host. It's good to know that the long years of captivity haven't impaired my judgment."

That's the most the bird has said to me so far, but one word in particular stands out. "Captivity?"

The bird makes a sound that's almost like a yawn. "You'd better go and have your dinner."

"I'm not really hungry," I say as I carefully sit on the edge of the bed. "I'd rather stay here and talk to you. Where were you held captive?" I ask, but the bird only sighs. Then Mrs. Martin calls me, and I know I have to go downstairs or else she'll come up to check on me.

"Go and nourish yourself. I'll rest while you're gone." The bird nestles against the soft towel and closes her eyes, which ends our conversation—for now.

I go downstairs and try to act as normal as possible. Mrs. Martin's got the baby carrier on the kitchen table, but Mercy's starting to fret. That's what she does before breaking into a full-blown wail. I'm about to ask if I can eat up in my room when Mrs. Martin asks me to rock the baby.

"She's been so unhappy today," Mrs. Martin says with a yawn. "Up all night and then she wanted to be held all day long. Poor thing."

I use my hand to rock the carrier back and forth, but the baby's screwing up her face, which means she's about to bawl.

"Not like that, D. Pick her up. She won't bite."

Bite? This kid doesn't even have teeth yet. It's my ear-drums I'm worried about. And what if her shrieks startle the bird—what if she decides to leave? Mrs. Martin's stand-ing at the stove watching me. I take a deep breath and pick up the wriggling baby.

As soon as I put her body against mine, Mercy becomes still. She whimpers a bit, but quiets down when I bounce her a little.

"That's it," says Mrs. Martin with a tired smile. "She likes you, D."

I can't imagine having to hold a cranky baby all day. "Maybe we should order in tonight," I suggest.

Mrs. Martin pushes herself off the counter and jumps into action. "No, no—you've been working hard at school all day. You deserve a home-cooked meal. It'll only take me a minute to warm this food up."

Mercy stays quiet for about two minutes, and then she starts to fret again. I keep bouncing her on my shoulder, and then I try walking around with her. But nothing I do seems to work, and before long she's screaming. Mrs. Martin turns off the stove and takes over.

"You can serve yourself, can't you, dear?"

"Sure," I say, only too happy to swap a bawling baby for a plate of hot food. "Uh—would it be OK if I ate up in my room? I sort of have a headache."

"That makes two of us," Mrs. Martin says with a sigh. The baby clutches Mrs. Martin's sweater in her tiny fists and buries her brown face in the old woman's wrinkly neck. Mercy quiets down after Mrs. Martin starts rubbing her back and humming softly in her ear. I watch them, and for just a moment I wish I were still small enough to be held like that. But Mercy's the baby—not me.

"Should I make a plate for you, too?" I ask.

Mrs. Martin shakes her head. "I'll eat later, once Mercy's gone to sleep."

I stand where I am, not sure it's really fair for me to leave Mrs. Martin alone with the baby—after all, she had to take care of Mercy all day. Mrs. Martin sees the guilt on my face and smiles. "Go on, dear. I'll be fine. You can come down later and show me your homework—not that you'll need my help. You're such a bright boy. We can have a cup of cocoa together."

"Yes, ma'am." I fix myself a plate and head upstairs, anxious to talk more with the bird. But when I reach my room, she's fast asleep, so I just eat my dinner and get my homework out of the way. When I take my plate back downstairs, everything's quiet. The can of cocoa's on the kitchen counter, but Mrs. Martin has fallen asleep in the rocking chair with Mercy resting peacefully in her arms.

For just a moment I feel like a ghost, an invisible intruder in some other family's home. I clean up the kitchen as quietly as I can, and then head back upstairs to check on the bird.

"Are you ready to retire?"

"You're awake!" There's something different about the bird, but I'm not sure it would be polite to say anything. Her feathers are no longer white. They look kind of dingy, like water-stained paper.

"I'll need a deeper sleep soon," she says, "but I wanted to talk to you first. I never thanked you."

"Thanked me? For what?"

"For saving me, of course."

"From the people who held you captive?"

"Yes. It's a long story, and I don't have the strength to tell it all tonight. I can, however, share some of my history." The bird suddenly spreads her wings and flutters over to my dresser. She nods at the vacated bed as if to tell me to get in.

I'm guessing this will be a bedtime story I'll never forget! I quickly change into my pajamas and slip into bed. Once I'm settled, the bird flies over and nestles against me like a cat.

"Are you glad you found me?" she asks.

"Sure!" I exclaim. "Nothing special ever happens to me—not special in a good way."

"You have endured much for one so young."

The bird doesn't look at me directly, but I get the feeling she's talking about my mother. "How do you know that?" I ask.

"I know many things about you. I can sense what is not said."

The only magical birds I've ever heard of were in books or movies. I never expected to find one in Prospect Park! And now it's here with me.

The bird looks up at me with her dark, sparkling eyes. "Many would have walked away—or tried to expose me for profit. But I knew you were different."

"Different how?"

"You have a tender heart."

I stiffen for just a moment, then relax as I realize the bird isn't calling me a wimp. She burrows against my neck, and I feel her tiny heart beating steadily.

"You should rest now. You'll need your strength for the task we must undertake."

"What task?" I ask with a yawn. I wasn't tired a moment ago, but now I'm having a hard time keeping my eyes open.

"When it is time, all will be revealed." The bird's voice sounds like a soothing lullaby. She reaches out a wing and strokes my cheek with the tips of her feathers.

I feel my eyes starting to close but manage to drowsily ask another question. "Why did you choose me?"

"You have nothing to lose," she croons.

Suddenly alert, I snap my head back and stare at the enchanting bird. "What?"

"No *one* to lose, I mean. I had to choose someone whose heart was free."

I want to object, to insist that I do have something—someone—to lose. But the bird is right. I like Mrs. Martin, and I appreciate her taking care of me and everything, but I'm not getting attached to her. And Mercy—well, even the visiting nurse said she can't form a bond with anyone because of the chemicals in her system. Poor kid. She came into this world with her heart already broken.

I let my head fall back onto the pillow. "So you picked me 'cause you thought I'd be more loyal?"

"Precisely. You're wise for your years, Dmitri."

"Call me D," I say.

"Why?"

"No one calls me Dmitri."

"Someone did...once."

My face heats up, and for just a moment I find myself wanting to crush this nosy bird. How could it know that my mother used to call me Dmitri?

"Great care was taken with your preparation," she says.

"Preparation?"

"Your education."

"Oh, I get it. My mom homeschooled me. She didn't trust the public schools, and we couldn't afford a private one."

"You don't belong at school."

"I don't belong anywhere, really."

"Everyone belongs somewhere," she says softly. "D?"

"Yes?"

"I am not what I appear to be."

"What do you mean?"

Instead of answering, the bird moves closer to the edge of the bed and silently morphs into a glowing yellow sphere.

I feel my tired eyes opening wide. "How'd you do that?"

In a deep male voice, it replies, "I am made of energy, D. I can sense what is in your heart and mind. Once I know what pleases you, I can adapt to suit your preferences."

"Are you—I mean, are you, like, an alien?"

"I must seem strange to you," the sphere says in its female voice before settling back into bird form.

"Uh—yeah! You're amazing. So…are you from another planet?"

"I am from…another realm."

"*Another realm.* This is so cool! And you came here and chose me—why?"

"You should rest, D." She reaches out her wing, but I pull back from her feathery touch.

"I'm not tired."

The bird doesn't sigh, but she lowers her eyes and seems resigned. "The journey we must undertake will require all the strength you can muster."

"Where are we going—back to your realm?"

"Yes. But first we must gather the dead."

"The dead!?" My heart begins to pound inside my chest. One second I am terrified, and the next I am filled with hope. Maybe this bird is an angel sent down from heaven! Mom must have sent her to get me, and now—

"Long dead, D." The bird looks at me, and there is kindness in her eyes along with an apology. "These souls have been waiting hundreds of years for me to return."

"You left them?" I say accusingly to hide my disappointment.

"Yes—but not by choice."

"Someone *made* you leave them behind?" I ask with suspicion.

"Yes. And those beings are out there still. They will hunt us, D."

The terror I felt a moment ago creeps back into my heart.

"As long as you stay close to me, I can keep you safe," she says reassuringly.

This time I don't pull away when the bird reaches out a protective silken wing. She drapes it across my cheek, and I feel myself falling asleep. "Why are they hunting you?"

This time the bird really does sigh. "All the dead are not dead, D. Souls that have suffered do not always find peace. They are restless, impatient. And sometimes... hostile."

Rest in peace. That's what the minister said at Mom's funeral. And RIP is sprayed on all the murals painted to honor the memory of those shot down in the street. I have just enough strength to ask one last question. "Where do they go—the souls that can't find peace?"

The bird touches her feathers to my lips, and suddenly I can't remember the question I just asked. I yawn and fall into a deep sleep.

7.

That night I dream that I am trapped in my room during a flood. Dark, murky water bubbles up from the drain in the basement and rapidly rises through the house. But just as the oily water oozes under my door, a brilliant star lights up the night sky and forces the water back downstairs and into the drain. I wake with a breathless gasp, but the bird brushes my face with her satiny feathers, and I immediately go back to sleep.

The next morning, Mrs. Martin beams at me like she always does before setting a bowl of oatmeal and steaming milk on the table. Mercy's gurgling contentedly in her carrier.

"Brown sugar or maple syrup?" Mrs. Martin asks.

I want to ask for maple syrup, but Mrs. Martin pays a lot for the small jugs they sell at the farmers' market. I don't feel right pouring it on thick like the cheap syrup my mom used to buy at the supermarket, and I like my oatmeal sweet. So instead, Perfect-me says, "Brown sugar, please."

Mrs. Martin brings the sugar bowl over to me. "You weren't in the basement last night, were you, D?"

"The basement? No, ma'am." Why would I go down there? It's damp and creepy and full of cobwebs and scurrying things.

"I came down this morning, and there was a dreadful draft—somehow the basement door came open during the night."

Just then icy air wafts into the room, and the hair on the back of my neck stands up. I glance over at the door leading into the basement, but it's shut tight and the bolt has been slid into place. I stir a lump of brown sugar into my oatmeal and try to remember more about the dream I had last night. Maybe it wasn't a dream after all. Could I have opened the door to the basement while sleepwalking? I've never walked in my sleep before, but these days a lot of things are happening to me that have never happened before.

After breakfast I rush upstairs to ask the bird about my bad dream, but when I reach my room, she's too tired to talk. "Keep me close," is all she says before closing her eyes and falling asleep once more. I carefully slip her into the inside pocket of my coat. Then I grab my book bag and head back downstairs. Before leaving for school, I check the bolt on the basement door and make a mental note to ask the bird more about whatever it is that's hunting her.

8.

It's Thursday. After my second tutoring session with Keem, I come out of the library and Nyla's there waiting for me. "About time," she says, rolling her eyes with pretend irritation. "What took you so long?"

"Sorry," I say. "I—I didn't know you were waiting for me."

Nyla pushes herself off the wall and nods at the golden bird she'd been leaning against. The façade of the library is covered with gold images of people and creatures from famous stories. Nyla chose the phoenix rising from the flames. "You said you were going to show me your bird-watching spot, remember?"

"Oh, yeah." I look at Keem and figure I better introduce him to Nyla. "You know Keem, right?"

Nyla gives Keem a once-over with her eyes and then says, "Hey."

"Hey," he replies without revealing a trace of the excitement I know he must be feeling inside.

"So…I guess I'll see you next week, Keem. On Tuesday."

Before Keem can reply, Nyla taunts him by saying, "I guess a jock like you is way too cool to look at birds."

Keem smiles without smiling. Only super cool kids can do that.

"If you're going over to the park, I'll hang with you for a while. I can't stay too late, though." Keem looks at me and says, "*Qadaa.*"

I nod, liking that he trusts me to remember the word's meaning. But apparently it's not a secret after all because Nyla says, "You're Muslim?"

Keem nods, but I see him grow tense, waiting for the joke or the insult that's to come.

"Which mosque do you go to?" Nyla asks, surprising us both.

"The one on Fulton Street. Know it?"

"Sure," Nyla replies as she leads us down the stairs and over to the street. "My girl goes to that mosque. Sanaa Jenkins—you know her?"

Keem nods. "Since we were little kids."

"She says you were a real hell-raiser back in the day."

Keem looks genuinely surprised. "Me? I don't think so. My dad doesn't play that. Ask D—he knows what my dad's like."

Nyla turns to me for confirmation. "I only met Mr. Diallo once, but...he seems pretty strict," I say.

"You don't know strict 'til you've met *my* dad," she says before darting across the street and nearly getting hit by a car.

Keem and I wait for the traffic to pass and catch up with Nyla. She's standing on the triangular island that divides the busy street. I grab hold of her bag to keep her from rushing out into traffic again.

I'm holding Nyla's bag, but Keem's the one holding her attention. They're still talking about all the things Sanaa Jenkins said about Keem. I hate to think it, but maybe Nyla has only been nice to me in order to get close to Keem. But Nyla's the prettiest girl in the whole school—she doesn't need my help to hook up with anyone. And she has to know Keem's into her...

Suddenly Nyla grabs my hand and pulls me into the street. "Move it or lose it, D!"

We run across the street, laughing at our recklessness. Keem's trapped on the island and has to wait for the light to change. While we're waiting for him, Nyla turns to me and says, "Do you mind if he comes with us? I can tell him to get lost if you want me to."

I'd much rather be alone with Nyla in the park, but Keem will be destroyed if Nyla tells him to go. "Keem's a good guy," I say. Not a ringing endorsement, but true.

Nyla watches Keem as the light changes and he does the jock-trot over to where we are. "Ready to spot some exotic birds?"

Before Keem and I can say anything, Nyla turns and heads into the park. We follow her knowing full well that Nyla's the most exotic creature we've ever seen.

I figure this is my chance to learn more about her, so I start with some small talk. "You've traveled a lot, huh?"

Nyla shrugs and then pulls her ringed fingers out of her pockets and counts off all the places she's been. I don't even have a passport, but Nyla must have stamps on every single page of hers.

"It's easy to get around when you live in Europe," she says. "Everything's close by, more or less."

"Is that how you learned to speak German?" asks Keem.

"*Natürlich, dumm.*" Nyla laughs at the confused looks on our faces. "I came here from Ramstein, but before that we moved around a lot. My dad's an Army engineer. Or was—he retired last year, so we came back here."

"Brooklyn must be kind of boring compared to Europe, huh?"

Nyla looks at me like I'm crazy. "Are you kidding? Brooklyn's the world." She throws out her arms and twirls around and around. Then, staggering dizzily, she says, "Everyone who's anyone lives here."

Keem's phone goes off, and he steps away to take the call. I catch Nyla watching him, trying to hear who he's talking to.

This is my chance—I've got Nyla all to myself. "So... what are you?" I ask.

Nyla's dimples vanish as the smile slides off her face. I rush on to fix my mistake. "I mean, are you, like, Goth? Or punk?"

Nyla's smile returns, and she flips her hair out of her eyes. "What you see is what you get, D. I'm *me*—take it or leave it."

Nyla watches me, her onyx eyes sparkling with unloosed laughter. She reaches out a hand and rubs it over my thick hair. I haven't had a haircut since I moved in with Mrs. Martin but plan to spend some of my tutoring money at the barbershop—soon.

"You'd look good with a faux-hawk," Nyla tells me.

"Can't—my mom would freak out," I say. Then I realize I've done it again—used the present tense for someone who's no longer present.

I try to look away, but Nyla sees the change in my face. "You and your mom don't get along?" she asks softly.

"We used to," I say, fingering the pink ribbon pin in my coat pocket. "But...my mom died a few months back. She had breast cancer." I press the sharp pink ribbon pin into my thumb, knowing Nyla will see me wince.

"Oh, God, D—I'm so sorry." Nyla reaches out and puts her hand on my face this time. I try not to sigh as the cold silver of her rings presses into my cheek. "It's just you and your dad then?"

I shake my head, and Nyla's hand falls away. "I never knew my dad."

"So who takes care of you now—your grandmother?"

I shake my head and decide not to tell Nyla about my bizarre lack of family. "I live with Mrs. Martin. She's my foster mother."

I never know what to do with other people's sympathy, but I like the way Nyla's looking at me now. Like she wishes she could give me something that would fill up the hole in my heart. Instead Nyla's puts her arms around me and holds me close for five full seconds. I know because I was counting!

Once Nyla takes her arms away, I feel sort of free inside—brave enough to admit the truth. "Sometimes I forget that my mom's gone. This past year feels like a bad dream that just won't end."

Nyla nods to show that she understands. "Some people say that life is just a dream—we only wake up when we die. The ancient Egyptians believed the dead weren't really dead. I think they were right—the dead live as long as we continue to say their names."

The dead aren't dead. That's what the bird said last night!

Nyla sees the amazed look on my face and smiles before making her own confession. "I still talk to my gran all the time. Dad dragged her all over Europe, but all she wanted was to come back home."

"Did she make it?" I ask.

Nyla's eyes seem to get a bit darker. "She passed while we were stuck in K-town."

"Is she buried in…K-town?"

"Kaiserslautern?" Nyla shakes her head. "She's on the mantle in my room—in an urn. We had her cremated." Nyla shrugs. "I didn't want to, but…it was easier than shipping the body overseas."

Finally Keem snaps his phone shut and comes over to where we are. "Sorry about that. Family drama."

"You gotta go?" I ask hopefully.

But Keem shakes his head. "Nothing I can do about it. My mother's upset because one of our neighbors saw my big sister and she wasn't wearing her headscarf." Keem shakes his head but can't stop himself from chuckling. "My dad's gonna hit the roof!"

Nyla puts a hand on her hip. "You got your sister's back, right?"

Keem looks at Nyla and knows he better say yes.

"No doubt. Nasira's the reason my dad lets me play ball. She made a list of all the Muslim players in the NBA—Hakeem Olajuwon, Kareem Abdul-Jabbar, Rasheed Wallace. Dad didn't stand a chance. My sister's going to make an awesome lawyer someday. Not wearing hijab is pretty serious for a Muslim girl—in my family, at least. But Nasira's probably already prepared her own defense."

I look at Keem and wonder if he's supposed to wear his kufi all the time, too. Then I turn back to Nyla and ask, "Would you ever cover your hair?"

"Hell yeah—it's not easy looking fabulous all the time." Nyla tosses her red bangs aside and winks at me. I look at Keem. He's trying not to grin like an idiot.

"So where are these beautiful birds, D?" Nyla scans the dull gray clouds in the sky.

"We have to cross the meadow," I tell her. "They prefer to nest in areas that are dense with trees." I lead them across the long meadow, a stretch of grass that's more yellow than green at this time of year. Now that Keem is back on the scene, Nyla's not so interested in me. I listen as she tells him about her friend Sanaa's sister, who sometimes goes out wearing a burka.

"She says it's like wearing an invisibility cloak. It makes her feel powerful. She doesn't have to worry about all those fools on the corner saying nasty stuff when she walks by. I swear, guys talk about us like we're nothing more than a piece of meat."

"You like being looked at," Keem says.

Stunned, I wait to see if Nyla's going to curse him out in German. She screws up her lips but then shrugs and says, "Maybe. I'm proud of who I am and how I look. But I got a right to be myself *and* be respected when I'm out in the street."

"True," Keem says with a nod. "But can you blame a brother for giving praise where praise is due?"

"Talking about my ass is *not* a compliment. Some negroes need to keep their 'praise' to themselves."

"Some girls like it," Keem counters.

Nyla sucks her teeth. "*Some girls* don't know any better. And *some girls* aren't trying to hear it—not from your kind."

She means not all girls like boys, but I'm not sure Keem gets the point Nyla's trying to make. I think about the group of "freaks" that hangs out with Nyla at lunch. Kids at school sometimes call Regine a "butch," and it was a boy who called Keem a "hottie." Could Nyla be one of those girls who's "not trying to hear it"? Maybe Keem's not my competition after all. Both of us might be barking up the wrong tree.

The three of us look up as a loud screech comes from above.

"Wow—is that an eagle?" Nyla asks.

"Red-tailed hawk," I tell her.

It veers off to the east, and we follow it instead of continuing across the meadow. The best bird sightings I've had were deeper in the park, away from the busy roads that run along the park's edge. But if Nyla wants to follow the hawk, I don't mind. At this time of day, there aren't a lot of people hanging around. Most kids our age have already gone home for dinner, and that leaves just a few runners, some dog walkers, and a cyclist or two. The days are getting longer, but it'll still be dark in a couple of hours. We cross the East Drive with no problem and head for the tree line.

There are paved paths that wind throughout the park, but I like the sound of dead leaves crunching under my feet. Plus I kind of want to see whether Nyla's with me or with Keem. So I veer off the path and into the woods, then wait a few minutes to see whether Nyla follows my lead. She doesn't. A girl in boots like those shouldn't be afraid of a little mud. But Nyla stays with Keem on the paved path.

They don't even pretend they're looking for birds—they only have eyes for each other.

Just as I'm starting to feel sorry for myself, I feel the bird stirring inside my coat and remember I'm not alone. I pull the zipper down a bit to check on her. "You OK in there? You slept a really long time."

The bird pokes her head out and looks around. Her alert eyes seem to glow. "Something's happening," she says.

The alarm in her voices pricks at my ears. "What? Where?"

"I don't know. Stay here. I'm going to investigate." And with that she flies up into the branches of a nearby oak tree. I watch as she hops from branch to branch, her head cocked to one side and then the next. Then, without any warning, she flies away.

"She said 'something's *happening*,' not 'something's *wrong*,'" I whisper to myself. Still, I felt more confident when the bird was sleeping soundly near my heart.

I glance over my shoulder to see what the two lovebirds are up to. Nyla's leaning up against a big tree, and Keem's standing a little too close to her, one hand pressed against the trunk above her head. I've seen guys do that with other girls at school. If someone did that to me, I'd feel trapped, but girls seem to dig that crap. I wonder how many girls have stood like that beneath Keem's arm. I want to believe Nyla's too smart to fall for that slick jock talk, but I can hear her laughing at his corny jokes. Keem thinks he's so smooth…

I'm so busy trying not to get caught staring at Keem and Nyla that I almost walk right into a tree. "Excuse me," I say and chuckle to myself. I take one step around the tree, and next thing I know, I'm flat on my face.

I lift my head above the dry brown leaves and look for the root I must have tripped over. Then something pinches my calf and I cry out—mostly in surprise.

"D—you all right?"

I hear Nyla's voice, but before I can even think of an answer, something *bites* my leg. I roll over and find the weirdest trap I've ever seen clamped down on my left calf. It looks like the jawbone of a wild animal or a really big dog, except that along with pointy teeth, the jaw is lined with curved bits of metal and the sharp talons of a large bird. I try to shake my leg free, but the jaw—or trap, or whatever it is—simply slides down my jeans until it reaches my ankle. Then it digs in. And *that's* when I scream!

"*D?*"

I can tell by the sound of her voice that Nyla's moving now, coming toward me. But then I feel a sharp tug, and suddenly I'm being dragged along the ground—slowly at first, like I'm a big, heavy fish that the person reeling me in can't handle. Then the pull gets stronger, and leaves and twigs start flying as I try to grab hold of anything that will slow me down. I try to call for help, but my head hits a rock, my teeth snap down on my tongue, and blood starts filling up my mouth. I feel like I'm drowning and falling at the same time.

I spit out a mouthful of blood and cry, "Help!"

Finally I manage to grab hold of a sapling. I flip over onto my stomach and see Nyla and Keem racing toward me. The jaw digs in deeper, and the sapling starts to bend. Just as my fingers lose their grip on the slender tree, Keem dives at me and grabs hold of my right hand. I reach for him with my other hand, and for a moment we're stuck in a tug of war. Keem swings his legs around and presses his feet into a big rock. Nyla searches for a heavy branch and holds it behind her head like a baseball bat. Problem is, there's no one to hit. It's like I'm being dragged along by a ghost!

Out of desperation, Nyla just starts beating the ground. Dead leaves fly up, and Nyla cries out, "There's a chain!" She drops the branch and reaches down to grab it. It's pulled taut and leads to a massive uprooted tree about twenty feet away. There's a gaping hole in the ground that's only partly covered by the snakelike roots of the dead tree. And down that hole is where I'm headed unless we find a way to break that chain.

Keem calls to Nyla, "We've got to get this thing off his leg! Get another branch—a smaller one we can use to pry it off."

Nyla frantically sifts through the dead leaves on the ground until she finds a strong, short stick. She rushes over to me and tries to wedge it between my ankle and the trap's jaws, but I can't keep still—first of all, it hurts! And second of all, I'm still being pulled toward that hole in the ground. Keem's tugging on me with all his might, but whatever it is just won't let go. Keem's yelling at Nyla, trying to tell her what to do. And Nyla's yelling at Keem, mostly because she's frustrated that the wedge won't work. I'm hollering because it feels like some beast is biting into my ankle with its razor-sharp teeth.

Suddenly, beneath our loud, panicked voices I hear a strange hissing. Actually, I don't really *hear* it—I *feel* it. It's like a cold, wet mist that slithers along the ground—and it's coming out of that hole. Something touches the sole of my shoe and then winds up my leg. I get goose bumps all over, and then I hear, "*It belongs to US.*"

I look over my shoulder so I can see where the voices are coming from, and then I yell even louder than before because something is coming out of the hole in the ground!

"Don't let it get me! Pull harder—pull harder!"

"I'm pulling as hard as I can!" shouts Keem. "You want me to pull your arms out?"

"But look! It's coming—it's coming for me!"

Nyla looks over at the uprooted tree and sees the gray mist oozing out of the hole in the ground. The horror I feel is now stamped on her face. Tendrils of fog unfurl like fingers and follow the length of chain that leads straight to us.

"*It's ours!*" The voices seem louder now that I've been shocked into silence.

"Oh—my—God." Nyla's words barely come out as a whisper, but somehow Keem hears her and follows her frightened gaze.

"What the..."

The ground beneath me starts to rumble. "*Give—it—BACK!*"

All of a sudden, a deafening cry comes from above. We all look up, expecting to find the hawk we saw earlier, but instead a blinding white light fills the late afternoon sky. We don't know whether to shield our eyes or plug our ears because a second later the hissing voices explode in an earsplitting shriek. And then...

Everything stops. The bright light dims, the angry voices grow silent, the jaw clamped on my ankle goes slack, and the sinister smoke seeps back underground.

Keem pulls the terrible trap off my leg and hurls it away in disgust. I see the flash of silver as Nyla reaches for my face. I try to speak, to thank my new friends, but instead I pass out in Nyla's arms.

9.

When I come to, Keem and Nyla are arguing over me. "He's bleeding pretty bad—we better take him to the hospital."

"And say what? 'Here's our friend. Some crazy beast-trap-chain thing tried to drag him underground while we were hanging out in Prospect Park.'" Nyla rolls her eyes. "They're not going to believe that!"

"So…we'll say a coyote did it! They've attacked kids before."

"In Brooklyn? If we blame a wild animal, he'll have to get rabies shots—the ER doctor will have to report it, his foster mother will get involved, maybe even ACS."

"No!" I mumble feebly. "They'll send me to the group home. I can't go back there…"

Nyla takes a deep breath. "Keem, take off your hoodie and give me your T-shirt."

"What for?"

"We have to make a bandage to stop the bleeding. Come on—hurry up!"

Keem does as he's told and pulls the baggy sweatshirt over his head. When his T-shirt comes off, I wait for Nyla to sigh and swoon over Keem's six-pack abs. But Nyla's too busy tearing Keem's yellow Lakers shirt into strips. I try not to cry out as Nyla ties them tightly around my ankle. Keem shivers and pulls his hoodie back on. For just a moment I think I see a hint of envy in his eyes. All of Nyla's energy is focused on *me*.

"Come on. We have to find a cab." Nyla puts her arm around my back and tries to help me stand.

"You go get the cab. I'll handle D." Keem gently pulls her away and then picks me up like I'm a sack of feathers. *Feathers*...where's the bird?

"Where are we going?" I ask.

"To my place," Nyla answers. "My mom's a nurse."

It would take us a long time to go back to the main entrance of the park, so Nyla leads us straight to the park's edge. A cast-iron fence topped with sharp spikes is meant to keep people out of the park, but there are gaps in the fence that give us access to the busy street. In two or three places, the iron bars have been twisted apart by cars that jumped the curb. Nyla rushes ahead of me and Keem and flags down a gypsy cab. A yellow cab would never stop for kids like us, but gypsy cab drivers in this city have seen it all, and before long we pull up in front of Nyla's brownstone. Keem reaches into his back pocket, but before he can pull out his wallet, Nyla flings a ten at the driver and tells Keem to bring me over to the basement door. "I'll come down and open it from the inside," she says before dashing up the stairs and letting herself in the front door.

In less than a minute Nyla opens the black iron grate under the stoop and lets us into her home. Keem's eyes open as wide as mine as he carries me down a long hallway and into a family room that looks like something out of an IKEA catalogue. Nyla's house is *nice*. I'm hoping I don't drip blood all over the place. I'm also hoping the bird will be able to find me here. "I've got to get back to the park," I mutter between my clenched teeth.

"Wait here. I'll go get my mom." Over her shoulder Nyla says, "Help yourself to whatever's in the fridge." She steps into the hallway and presses an intercom button on the wall. "Mom?"

Keem peeks inside the mini fridge tucked under the bar, but like me, he's afraid to touch anything. "You met her mom before?"

"No." Why would he think that? "You?"

Keem shakes his head and wanders over to the entertainment center, which includes a flat-screen television that practically covers the entire wall. Keem whistles with appreciation. "Imagine watching the game in here!"

"Mom!" Nyla tries the intercom one more time, and then goes over to the foot of the stairs and hollers, "MOM!"

Footsteps overhead tell us that Nyla's mother is home after all. "Nyla? Why are you yelling like that?"

Nyla changes her tone of voice. "Hey, Sachi. Listen—I need a favor."

We hear the soft slap of slippers as Nyla's mother comes downstairs. "What kind of favor?"

"A friend of mine got hurt in the park. I need you to fix him up."

"What happened?"

Keem frowns and looks at me. Will Nyla tell her mother the truth?

"He—uh—we think he stepped on an old trap. You know those illegal traps they use to catch bears and stuff. Tore his ankle up pretty bad."

The pause that follows is long enough for us to know that Nyla's mother isn't buying that explanation. "Why would there be a metal trap in the park? And why didn't you take him to the hospital?"

Nyla sighs impatiently. "He doesn't have health insurance, OK? Listen, Sachi, I don't have time to chat right now. He's in a lot of pain."

There is another pause, and Keem and I have to strain our ears to hear what's said next. "You know I lost my license. Why are you doing this, Nyla?"

"Because I have no choice. He's just a kid, and he needs your help. You owe me, Sachi. You know you do."

Nyla's mother says nothing for a long moment. Finally she says, "Where is he?"

Nyla leads her mother down the hallway and into the family room. I shift on my barstool and try not to look too pathetic. Keem stands next to me, his hands jammed into the front pocket of his hoodie.

"This is Keem, and this is D. His left ankle's pretty messed up. You guys, this is my stepmother, Sachi."

"I'm your stepmother now, am I? You called me 'Mom' a moment ago."

"Relax, Sachi. It's just easier this way. I don't have time to explain our sordid family history."

I wouldn't mind hearing that story, and judging from the look on Keem's face, he wants to hear it, too. Sachi is a pretty Asian woman. She's about Nyla's height, and she has bobbed black hair that refuses to stay tucked behind her ear.

To Nyla she says, "Get me some gloves."

Nyla goes around the bar and opens a couple of drawers before returning with a pair of latex gloves. Sachi rolls up my pant leg and gently unwinds the makeshift bandage. I wince as air pours over the gaping wound. Sachi purses her lips and peers at my ankle. "This was no trap. An animal did this." She frowns and begins pulling off the tight plastic gloves she just put on. "He'll need a rabies shot. Let's get him to the ER."

Nyla steps in front of Sachi to block her exit. "It wasn't an animal."

"I know a bite mark when I see one, Nyla."

"He was cut with a claw, but it wasn't on an animal, OK? Look—I can't explain it right now. Just clean him up. We have to get out of here before Daddy gets home."

"Are you in trouble again? Christ, Nyla, we just moved here…"

"I *know* you're not going to lecture *me* about getting into trouble. I saw you on the computer yesterday. And I know you use my laptop when I'm not around."

Sachi's face loses most of its color and then blushes hot red. "I—I was just checking my e-mail."

"Oh, really? Well, I'm sure Daddy will be thrilled to know you're already back online."

Sachi's lower lip starts to tremble. "You can't keep doing this, Nyla. We're family."

"You're right, Sachi. We are. And that's why you're going to help my friend."

Sachi rolls her lips together and looks at the floor. Then she goes into a nearby bathroom and opens a cabinet. She comes back with a bunch of medical supplies and sets them on the counter next to me. To Keem and Nyla she says, "Hold his hands and try to keep him still." To me, in a kinder voice, she says, "Try to be a brave boy, OK? I don't have any anesthesia, so just squeeze their hands if the pain's too much for you to handle."

"I can handle it," I say, but then I squeeze the heck out of their hands as the alcohol spills into the wound. It gets worse when the needle starts sliding in and out of my skin.

"Dang, D—I can't play ball if you break my hand!"

I look up at Keem and almost manage to laugh.

Nyla reaches over and pulls my hand away from Keem's. "Hold both of *my* hands, D. I can take it."

I don't have to glance at Keem to know he wishes he'd kept his mouth shut.

Finally Sachi puts the needle down and tells me she's done. She gently squeezes my knee and says, "I'll give you something for the pain. Nyla, get him something to eat. He can't take pain medication on an empty stomach."

"You were really brave, D. I know that must have hurt a lot." Nyla smiles at me, then lets go of my hands and goes behind the bar to look for some snacks.

"Potato chips?"

I nod my head, but Sachi comes back into the room and says, "Keep looking."

Nyla pulls bag after bag of snacks out of the cupboard. When she calls out, "Peanut butter pretzels," Sachi nods and Nyla brings them over. She sees Keem eyeing the other bags on the counter and tells him to help himself. I'm told to eat five pretzels before swallowing the pill Sachi sets on the bar next to a glass of water.

"You going to tell me what's going on?" she asks us.

Nyla doesn't exactly shake her head. She just nibbles at a pretzel and avoids her stepmother's worried eyes.

"What should I tell your father when he gets home?"

Nyla shrugs. "Just tell him I'm out with friends." Nyla grabs her jacket and turns to us. "You guys ready to go? You can take the snacks, if you want. And, Keem—grab us a couple of bottles of water, why don't you."

Keem does as he's told and puts a bag of chips and some water into his book bag. Nyla tries to get around her stepmother, but Sachi doesn't budge. Nyla sighs and says, "Tell Daddy I'll be home soon. Before dark." Then Nyla surprises us all by leaning in and kissing her stepmother on the cheek. "Thanks for helping us out, Mom."

Sachi's cheeks flush again, but she steps aside and lets us pass. At the door she calls after Nyla, "Be careful, sweetheart."

Keem's the first one of us to talk. "So...where's your real mom?"

"'Real mom'? Sachi's the only mother I've ever known. My birth mom bounced when I was four."

"Oh, sorry."

Nyla shoots Keem a look that says, "I don't want your pity."

Keem tries again. "I mean, your stepmom's cool."

Nyla glances over her shoulder. Her stepmother is watching us from the parlor window. Nyla waves and then turns back to us. "Yeah, Sachi's all right."

"Did you really have to blackmail her like that?" I ask.

Nyla just shrugs. "I wouldn't have told on her—she knows that. My dad's kind of hard-core. Sachi and I look out for each other."

"Why can't she use your computer?" Keem asks.

"When we lived on base, Sachi had a little problem with Internet gambling." Nyla pauses for effect then says, "Let's just say my college savings account ain't what it used to be. But enough of my family drama—where exactly are we heading?"

"Back to the park," I say.

Keem bars my way with his never-ending arm. "Hold up, D. If you mean the park where you nearly got killed a little while ago, NO WAY!"

"But I have to go back!"

"Why?" asks Nyla.

I look at Nyla, then Keem, and try to decide what to say. "I—I left something behind."

"I brought your book bag," Nyla says.

"I know—and thanks. But...there's something else. *Someone* else."

Keem laughs a little. "You got an invisible friend I don't know about?"

Nyla reaches across me and smacks Keem on the arm. "Quit playing, Keem. D's serious." She turns her beautiful black eyes on me. "Who's missing, D?"

A few hours ago, I wouldn't have called these two my friends, but now—after what we've just been through—I feel like I owe them the truth. There's an ice cream shop at the end of the block. I lead us over there and sit down on one of the wooden benches. In the summertime this place is always packed, but it's still too cold out for people to line up for ice cream. Nyla and Keem sit on either side of me.

After taking a deep breath, I say, "Yesterday I found this bird. I thought it was injured, so I brought it home with me." Keem's looking at me like I'm crazy, so I keep my eyes locked on Nyla. "But it turned out not to be a bird at all."

"What was it, D?" she asks in the slow voice reserved for little kids.

I try not to get irritated. Would I believe this story if it wasn't already happening to me? "It was a being from another realm," I say calmly.

"Psssshhhhh." Keem gets up from the bench and runs his hand over his shaved head. "I ain't got time for this."

"Then leave!" says Nyla with much attitude.

Keem looks at me the way I sometimes look at Mercy when she's getting all of Mrs. Martin's attention. "It's true!" I yell at him. "You think I'm making this up?" I grab my pant leg and lift it to show the bandage on my ankle. "You think that…*thing* was after *me*? It was after the bird!"

"Right—the bird that's not a bird. I think you need to take your meds, D."

Nyla flies to her feet. "You know what, Keem? Just go. I thought you were someone decent—I thought you weren't like all those other guys."

"I *am* decent—but I'm not crazy! You believe this crap?"

Nyla puts her hands on her hips. "I was *there*, Keem. Something tried to get D."

Keem can't deny that, so he tries to come up with something else. He turns to me. "OK, so where was this bird while you were getting dragged across the park?"

"It flew away just before the thing grabbed me." Keem rolls his eyes, so I rush on and add, "But it knew something was wrong!"

"So it flew off to safety and left you to fend for yourself? Some friend," he says.

I don't have an answer for that. Nyla sits down on the bench and starts rubbing my back. Even she's at a loss for words. Then I hear a familiar voice in my ear.

"He's right. It was a foolish mistake—they set up a decoy on the far side of the meadow. As soon as I got there, I realized what I'd done. I'm so sorry, D."

I spin around and find the bird perched on the top rung of the bench. Her feathers are changing color again, but I'm too relieved to care. I pull her to me and hold her close to my heart. "You're safe! I was worried about you."

"The nether beings cannot harm me. They hunt me only so that they may keep me from my mission."

"*Our* mission," I say and lean down to press my lips against the bird's head. I'm filled with such joy that I forget Nyla and Keem are watching me. "Uh—I want you to meet my friends."

Keem and Nyla are staring at me with their eyes open wide. At first I wonder if maybe I'm the only one who can hear the bird speak. Then the bird turns to face them and says, "I must thank you two as well. You made a valiant effort to save my host."

At first, Nyla and Keem are too shocked to say anything. I try to reassure them that what they're seeing and hearing is real. "I know it must seem weird, but…"

Nyla reaches out a hand and touches the bird's orange feathers. "Is it—a parrot?"

Instead of answering, the bird silently morphs into a purring orange tabby cat. Nyla freezes, then lets her fingertips trails across the cat's soft fur. "How'd it do that?" she asks me.

"It can tell what you like and don't like," I explain. "You try, Keem."

He steps forward and reaches out his hand to pet the cat, but it shape-shifts into a basketball.

"No way," Keem says softly. He raps his knuckles on the ball but doesn't try to take it from me.

"D prefers this form," she says, turning herself back into a bird. "Do you need further proof of my abilities?"

Keem frowns, still unconvinced. "If you're so special, why didn't you help D when that...*thing* was trying to drag him underground?"

The bird turns to look up at me. "Did you see anything remarkable while you were in the park?"

To my surprise, I laugh a little. "Aside from the crazy trap biting into my leg?"

"And the creepy smoke thing crawling toward us?" adds Nyla.

The bird nods solemnly. "The earth—and all that lies above and below its surface—that is their terrain. My domain—"

"Is the sky!" I exclaim. Suddenly it all makes sense to me. "It wasn't a hawk we heard—it was you, wasn't it?"

The bird nods and modestly lowers her eyes. "The nether beings detest light."

Keem speaks up. "Wait a minute—you were that flash of light in the sky?"

"So you did try to help D," Nyla says, relieved.

The bird looks at Nyla. "He is my host," she says simply. "If I lose D, my mission will fail."

Keem kicks a crushed soda can into the gutter. "D's just a kid—why does he have to be mixed up in *your* mission?"

Nyla nods reluctantly. "He is kind of young."

"Hey—I can speak for myself! And I *want* to help the bird. She has to gather the dead—they've been waiting a really long time!"

Nyla and Keem stare at me with their mouths hanging open. I want to explain, but realize I don't really know much more about the mission.

The bird flutters up to my shoulder and says to them, "Again, I thank you for the service you have rendered my host." To me she says, "We should leave now."

Keem steps forward and points at my leg. "He's hurt, you know. Your 'nether beings' nearly tore his leg off!"

The bird flutters its wings and settles on my knee. "Are you in pain?"

"A little, but Nyla's stepmother fixed me up." Suddenly I feel a tickling sensation in my knee. I force myself not to laugh as the funny feeling moves down my calf and settles on my wounded ankle. "The pain's gone!" I whisper with awe. After the bird flies back to the bench rung, I lift up my pant leg and unwind the bandage Sachi carefully wrapped around my ankle. The wound is no longer bleeding—in fact, it no longer looks like a wound! All I see are faint zigzag marks where the stitches used to be. "You did that, didn't you?"

The bird is less modest this time. "My host must be healthy and whole," she says proudly. "Ready?"

"Ready. Where are we going?" I ask.

"Back to the park—and we must get there before sundown."

Keem blocks our path. "I don't think so, bird—do you even have a name?"

"I do. You may call me Nuru."

"Well, D's with *us* now, Nuru."

Nyla steps between them and tries to soften Keem's stance. "What Keem means to say is, we really can't let you put D in danger again."

"He won't be in danger if we reach the park as soon as possible."

I unzip my jacket, tuck the bird inside, and then turn to Nyla and Keem. "I appreciate what you guys have done for me, but...I think I better do this alone."

"Do what—get yourself killed?" asks Keem.

Instead of feeling grateful for this brotherly concern, anger flashes inside of me. "What do you care? You can always get another math tutor. A week ago you didn't even know who I was—and didn't *want* to know."

Nyla touches my arm, and I turn to face her. "What about now, D? What about that scene in the park—can you really blame us for being worried about you?"

"No. But I *have* to do this. I can't explain—it's just something I have to do." I push past them and walk away with my heart thudding in my chest. Part of me hopes they'll follow us to the park, but then I remember how cozy Keem and Nyla were getting before. "They're probably glad to be rid of me," I mutter under my breath. Still, I can't stop myself from glancing over my shoulder when I reach the end of the block. Nyla and Keem are sitting on the bench absorbed in their own conversation. When they see me watching them, they get up and head off in the opposite direction. "Fine, forget them," I mutter.

The sky is growing dark, so I walk quickly, and before long we reach the park. I open my jacket, and Nuru pops out and settles herself on my shoulder.

"We need to get to the lake," she says. "Try to stay close to the bridge—once the signal's been sent, we'll need to slip underground as quickly as possible."

Determined to avoid the east side of the park where I was attacked, I head across the meadow knowing I can reach the Lullwater Bridge by cutting through the ravine.

I already know that Nuru has a way of making me obey her will, but I decide now's as good a time as any to find out just what it is we're about to do. "Are we going after the nether beings?"

"No!" she cries, sounding genuinely alarmed. "We must avoid them at all costs. My flare has no doubt sent them deep into the earth. But they will surface again once the signal reaches them."

"If we're trying to avoid them, why are you sending them a signal?"

"The signal is for the waiting souls. They must prepare for our departure."

"Because we're taking them back to your realm?" I ask.

"Yes. They've waited long enough to go home."

I keep quiet for a while, thinking about Nuru's plan and the unlikely turn my life has taken. If I had found Nuru a few months ago, could she have cured my mother's cancer? But Nuru said she chose me because I had no one to lose. So I guess Mom had to die before any of this could happen to me.

Lullwater winds like a snake, but it's really the tail end of the big lake at the bottom of the park. There's boating in the summer, though the boathouse is now an Audubon Center. I used to go there with my mom. There's a café inside, and in the summer folks sit out by the water and feed the ducks. Mom used to say the boathouse reminded her of Venice with its white pillars and fancy lampposts. I've never been to Italy, so I just took her word for it. The boathouse and the bridge definitely look like they're from another time.

Having waterways in the park is important because it creates habitat for all kinds of birds. If I were a migrating bird, I'd definitely stop here. There's a stream that feeds the lake, making a little waterfall at one end. Large rocks embedded in the ground serve as steps that lead down to the water's edge. I carefully follow these over to Lullwater Bridge.

Nuru starts shifting from one foot to another. I can sense that she's about to take flight, so I quickly ask, "Will they mind that I'm coming, too? The souls of the dead, I mean. They won't be mad or anything, will they?"

Nuru settles on my shoulder once more. "Mad? They will sing your praises, D! These souls are nothing like the nether beings. They embraced death when it came to them, and have waited patiently for this release. They will bless you for ensuring the return to their homeland."

"Why are the nether beings so different? Don't they want to go home, too?"

Nuru sadly shakes her head. "They do not recognize my realm as their place of origin. They suffer under a cruel delusion that traps them in a kind of purgatory. The nether beings are souls that do not seek release. They cling to the earth on which they died."

"What? You mean the nether beings died here—in the park?"

"Long ago this was a battlefield, D."

"I know—the British fought the patriots here during the Revolutionary War. There's a boulder over there with a plaque on it."

"There are two boulders and two plaques, and both are portals into the netherworld. One doorway leads to their realm, and the other leads to mine."

"So…once we're underground, we won't see them—will we?"

"It isn't likely. With the aid of allies, I was able to construct a network of secret tunnels during the long years of my captivity."

"Allies? Why didn't they help you escape?"

"They were animals—burrowing creatures. Only a human can be my host."

I used to think a host was someone who invited you over to their house for dinner. But I'm starting to realize that Nuru uses the word to mean something else. I'm about to ask her about my host duties when Nuru whispers in my ear, "We're not alone."

I freeze and quickly scan the ground for another trap. Then I take a deep breath and look over my shoulder. Nyla and Keem are standing on the far side of the lake.

11.

Nuru hops off my shoulder and into my hands. "You have to stay with me from now on, D."

"You mean *you* have to stay with *me*," I say. I know all too well what can happen when Nuru flies off, even if it's just to look around. I can feel Nyla and Keem staring at me, but I turn away from their gaze and try to reassure Nuru of my loyalty. "I'm not going anywhere."

"We are bound to one another, D. From this point forward, even if you let go, I will not."

Nuru pauses and looks at me as if trying to speak with her eyes. I feel a chill go up my spine, but I still nod to show that I understand.

"For the moment you may go and join your rather persistent friends. They are also bound to you, it seems," she says. "I must prepare to send the signal that will wake the dead."

Nuru lifts herself up into the sky and flies to the center of the lake. I slowly skirt the shore trying to think of what I'll say to Nyla and Keem. Keem's got his hands jammed in the front pocket of his hoodie. Nyla's arms are folded across her chest. Neither of them looks happy to see me.

On the grassy slope next to the boathouse is a big pile of gray paving stones. The Parks Department must be planning to extend the café's patio. I try to kick one of the heavy stones with my foot, but it hardly moves. Without looking up I say, "You should be at home. Isn't it time for evening prayer?"

"I'm allowed to miss prayer if I'm saving someone's life."

Keem looks more like he wants to personally *end* my life, but I accept his answer with a nod.

Nyla looks mad, too, but I think I can hear a hint of sadness in her voice. "So this is it, huh? You're just going to leave and go to this other…realm?"

I kick at the paving stone again and this time manage to make it roll over. "Why not? I mean, I told you what my life is like. My mother's dead, I don't even know who my father is, and my foster mother won't miss me—she's got another poor kid to take care of. What have I got to lose?"

"Uh—how about your life? Or don't you care about that?" asks Keem.

I shrug. "Nuru needs me."

We all look out over the lake and wait to see what will happen next. For a long time, Nuru hovers above the water with her wings beating fast like a hummingbird. Then she morphs into a glowing orange orb and, like the setting sun, slowly sinks toward the surface of the lake. The orb spins rapidly until it touches the water, and then it stills and the air all around us throbs as if someone has struck a giant gong. The water ripples outward in gentle waves, lapping against the shore just inches from our feet.

Keem puts a hand to his chest. His diaphragm must be vibrating just like mine. "Whoa…what was that for?" he asks.

"You don't want to know," I answer.

"Try me," says Keem.

"She's raising the dead."

"Great," says Nyla sarcastically. "I wouldn't want to miss this party."

The orange sphere rises up into the sky and begins spinning once more. In the distance, the actual sun shoots streaks of red across the sky.

"'Red sky at night, sailor's delight.' My Gran used to say that whenever she saw a pretty sunset," Nyla says.

We're so busy admiring the sky that we don't notice the gray mist slithering past our feet. Suddenly one of the heavy paving stones rolls past us and splashes into the lake. We turn and watch with dread as the sinister mist seeps into the big pile of paving stones.

"Oh, shit," says Nyla. "What now?"

Before Keem or I can answer, a loud rumbling erupts from the center of the pile and the paving stones begin to move. They seem to swirl at first, but then the brick-like stones rise in the air and come together to form a massive body that's at least twice as tall as Keem. I expect to hear this beast roar, but it can't—because it has no head! The stones that make up its limbs seem to be held together by the weblike mist, and we all jump back as a powerful stone arm takes a swing at us. The stone beast staggers, then finds its balance and reaches out—for me!

Nyla shoves me as hard as she can. "Run, D—RUN!"

I fall back into the lake, soaking my feet. My body wants to flee, but I can't go anywhere without Nuru. I try to scan the sky while keeping an eye on the headless stone monster. "I can't—I have to find Nuru!"

Keem looks like he's about to curse me out. Then he darts around the stone beast and starts jumping up and down, waving his arms over his head. "Hey—over here! Hey!"

Even though the beast has no head, it clumsily swivels to face Keem. "*Get the boy!*" It follows the hissed command and takes one lumbering step forward, then another.

"Grab the bird and get out of here!" Keem snarls at me. Then he takes off with the stone beast in pursuit.

I search the sky for Nuru and finally spot her descending from the clouds on flame-colored wings. Nuru seems to be moving in slow motion now, and I anxiously pace the shore until she finally comes within reach. I wade into the water, reach out my hands, and pull her warm body close to my own.

"Let's go, D!"

I tuck Nuru inside my jacket, then turn and run into the woods with Nyla. We can hear Keem yelling, "Over here! Follow me, you stupid hunk of rock!" But when we turn to look, the stone beast is no longer following Keem. It's lumbering after us!

Nyla grabs my sleeve and yanks me into the dense forest, but the creature only thins itself out, dropping excess stones and picking up dead branches to use as limbs. It's moving faster and faster, weaving through the trees, breaking apart and reassembling itself instead of going around the big trees like us. Heavy paving stones whiz past us as the beast hurls parts of itself in order to knock us down.

I turn to see how quickly it's gaining on us and trip over a fallen branch. Nyla screams at me to get up, then grabs the collar of my coat and hauls me up off the ground. For the first time, I realize just how strong she is.

"Come on—this way. Let's see how it handles stairs."

But just as we start to dash up the stairs that lead out of the ravine, the stone beast makes a giant leap and knocks us both into the gully. When I finally stop rolling downhill and manage to look up, my heart jumps into my throat.

The stone beast has got Nyla pinned to a tree. She is struggling to break free, but its fist of stone is pressing her into the trunk several feet off the ground. With its other hand, it reaches down and grabs something dark and thin off the forest floor.

"No!" I cry, but the beast ignores me and thrusts a spiked iron fence rail at Nyla. Already pinned to the tree, there's little she can do to avoid the spear. But with no eyes to see with, the creature's aim is off and the first jab enters the tree—not Nyla.

"STOP! Don't—you'll hurt her!" I yell.

The beast ignores me, plucks the fence rail out of the tree, and thrusts it at Nyla once more. This time the spike pierces her shoulder and lodges in the tree. Nyla screams in pain.

I frantically search inside my coat and pull out the bird. She shimmers in my trembling hand. "Look—look what I've got! I have it—I have it right here. And I'll give it to you." My voice cracks as a sob inches up my throat. "Just don't hurt her—don't hurt my friend."

Nuru burns in my hand like a flame, and I hold my arm high like a torch in the gathering dark. The beast turns toward me, its free hand reaching for the bird.

"NO! You have to let her go first. Put her down and then I'll give you the bird."

The beast rocks back on its heels, unsure what to do. Then the vicious hissing returns, and the beast pulls the spike out of Nyla's shoulder. She drops to the ground, moaning in pain.

Now the beast turns to me, but before I can figure out how to give it the bird, I feel a burning sensation in my hand. Suddenly Nuru is so hot I'm forced to unfurl my fingers. She hovers in the sky like a brilliant star just a few inches above my raised arm. I have to shield my eyes from the bright light, but I can still hear her say, "I'm sorry, D. It is as I feared. Your heart is no longer free. Forgive me."

Before I can say anything, Nuru rises up into the sky and then flies straight at me. I close my eyes and turn away but still feel the impact as Nuru slams into my body.

"Ooomph!" I feel like someone has just knocked all the air out of me. I sink to my knees, struggling to breathe. Then a warm, tingly sensation spreads all over my body. It's like being wrapped in a blanket of light. Red sparks dance around me like fireflies in summertime. What has Nuru done?

"Bring the boy to us!"

Nyla hears the hissing voices and drags herself over to me. She grabs my hand and says, "Go, D—run!"

I squeeze her fingers, letting some of this new warmth enter into her as well. "I can't run anymore," I say, but it doesn't sound like my usual voice. It sounds like Nuru.

"Don't give up," Nyla whispers through her tears.

"I have to," I say, though I want nothing more than to stay and help Nyla the way she helped me. I peel Nyla's fingers away and try not to watch as she clutches her wound and curls into a ball. Nyla's sobs follow me as I walk away, the spiked fence rail poking into my back as the stone beast prods me forward.

I hear Nyla moaning behind me, and then, with all the strength she can muster, Nyla screams, "KEEM!"

I look back and see a flash of red in the trees. This time it's not a cardinal—it's Keem's red hoodie. I almost choke with relief when I see Keem break out of the woods and sprint toward Nyla. He's strong—he'll get her out of here and make sure she's OK.

The sharp spike digs into my back again, and I stumble on toward my own fate.

12.

I trudge up East Drive hoping that a passing jogger or car will spot me and call the police. But tonight the park seems as if it has been abandoned by the living. Even the animals in the park zoo are silent. The biggest full moon I have ever seen stares down at me like an unblinking eye.

The stone beast forces me to march through the gap between two hills called Battle Pass. That's where American soldiers tried to stop the enemy's advance by blocking the road with a massive oak tree. It was a pretty good strategy except that the British secretly circled around them at night and trapped the patriots. We eventually won the war, but we lost that first Battle of Long Island. It's all on a plaque attached to a big rock—I've read it a hundred times. The boulder's embedded in the steep hill on the west side of the road. That must be the portal Nuru told me about because that's *not* where I'm heading now.

As darkness descends, it becomes clear that our destination is the other boulder—a smaller white rock set a few feet back from the road on the east side. It too has a plaque on its front, and as we approach, the hissing voices say, *"Bring him in."*

Nothing should surprise me at this point, but I'm still amazed when the engraved bronze plaque swings open like a door. A blast of stale, earthy air blows over me, and I'm immediately reminded of the basement at Mrs. Martin's house. I barely have a moment to wonder if she's missing me before the spike prods me forward again. I crawl into the small opening but can't force myself to descend the stairs that lead down into total darkness.

Suddenly the stone beast sways and starts to crumble. I nearly tumble down the stairs as several heavy paving stones roll past me. To steady myself, I grab hold of the tangled roots that cover the stairway's earthen walls like hair. Within a few noisy seconds, the stone beast is reduced to a pile of rubble that nearly covers the white boulder. I hear a sharp click and realize the plaque-door has just closed. I sigh and blink back fresh tears. No one will find me now.

Don't worry, D. I am with you.

I press myself into the dirt wall and try to see through the darkness. "Who's there?"

Can you not feel me? Look inside your heart, D. You are not alone.

I unzip my coat, pull out my collar, and peer inside my shirt. A soft red glow is coming from within my chest. "Nuru?"

You must listen for my commands, D. The nether beings will play on your fear, but they will not harm you. Have faith in me, and I will keep you safe.

I think of the stone beast thrusting that spike into Nyla and wonder what will stop the nether beings from doing the same to me. But I can't afford to doubt Nuru now. "OK," I say. "I trust you."

You must communicate with me using your mind instead of your voice.

How can I talk without using my voice? I just nod instead and take a deep breath before cautiously inching down the stairs. There are no lights, but somehow the glow within my chest pushes back the darkness enough for me to see my way forward. After a few more steps, I hear eerie laughter coming from below. I freeze, but Nuru urges me on.

We cannot retreat. They are celebrating my capture, but theirs is a false victory. The nether beings can no longer take human form. They can only manipulate surface materials.

I open my mouth to respond, but then remember I have to communicate with my thoughts. I form a question in my mind. *Surface materials?*

Things that can be found above ground—inanimate objects.

"Like that trap and chain!" I exclaim, then clamp my hand over my mouth. *Sorry,* I say without sound. It's going to be hard learning to speak with my mind.

The stone beast was also propelled by their malice. While I was their captive, they were able to maintain their human form. But now—to you—they will seem monstrous. Remember, D—they are only shadows that fear the light you have within. Be brave!

I press myself against the damp wall and try to breathe deeply to slow my racing heart. I can hear voices coming from below. Several men are arguing angrily—but they're not men, they're the dead—and Nuru called them "monsters"! Above ground, their collective voices sounded like a hissing snake, but now that I am underground, the nether beings sound like regular human beings.

"Where is he?"

"Drag him in here! Who's he to keep us waiting like this?"

"Patience, men, patience! He hasn't the heart of a soldier."

The men laugh at the suggestion that I'm a coward. They quiet down after a while, and I realize the last speaker must be their leader.

"Come in, boy, come in!"

I move toward his booming voice even though I know his welcome is insincere. When I reach the bottom of the stairs, I find myself in a large cavern. A gust of air blows past me, and suddenly three torches ignite and fill the space with orange light and wavering black shadows. The cavern is actually a junction, an open space circled by gaping black holes that must lead to other tunnels or stairways. Tangled roots hang from the ceiling, and wriggling worms burrow in and out of the damp earthen walls. Then I look closer and realize the worms aren't moving through soil—they're moving through the decomposing flesh of the dead!

I reach up and cover my nose with my hand, expecting to be overwhelmed by the stench of rotting flesh. But Nuru was right—the dead are like shadows, glimmering glimpses of the men they used to be. Soldiers who died in battle more than two hundred years ago shouldn't be walking and talking—and looking—like this. Those at the back of the cavern appear to be skeletons while the ones closer to me have enough flesh on their bones to appear more like corpses. I can even see the fatal wounds that killed some of them—a bayonet gash across the abdomen, a bullet wound in the temple.

To my surprise, they aren't wearing uniforms—just drab-colored long coats over plain shirts and pants that end at the knee. Some have stockings and shoes with buckles, others wear heavy leather boots that reach their breeches. All have long hair that's pulled back in a ponytail. In my mind, I imagined all Revolutionary soldiers looked like George Washington in his powdered wig, but this motley crew looks anything but dignified.

There are about a dozen nether beings altogether, and they all seem determined to get as close to me as they can. I'm not sure if they really can't touch me—Nuru said they could only move objects around—but I sure don't want to find out! As they press forward, I creep back toward the stairs until their leader calls his men to attention. A couple of centuries haven't diminished these soldiers' sense of discipline, and they fall in line immediately.

The leader proudly surveys his men as they stand at attention, their eerie eyes glued to the wall instead of feasting on me. "At ease, men," he says next, and they widen their stance and clasp their hands—what's left of them—behind their backs. I take this opportunity to look around the room. It's filled with items you'd expect to find in the park's lost-and-found bin—I see a few baseball bats and tennis rackets in one corner, stacks of newspapers and tattered paperback books in another, and two umbrellas, a shovel, and several lawn chairs are arranged around a three-legged plastic table that's propped up by a walking cane.

I jump when the leader suddenly speaks to me. "So, my boy. Where is it?"

"W-where is what?" I stammer.

"Don't fool with me, boy. You know what we're looking for."

I wait to hear Nuru's voice inside my head, but all I hear is the loud thudding of my heart. "Uh—if you mean the bird…it left. I tried to offer it to—to your rock servant thing, but it flew away before I could hand it over."

"You're lying," says the captain.

"I'm not!" I take off my jacket and turn around so they can see that I'm not hiding anything. "See?"

"Take off your clothes, nigger," snarls one of the soldiers. "Make him strip, Captain!"

"Yes!" the others shout as a chorus, swarming around me like a mob. "Strip, strip, strip!"

This time the captain makes no effort to rein his men in. I realize I have no choice but to obey and so start unbuttoning my shirt. I turn away to hide the glow in my chest, but to my relief, the light has dimmed completely. My cheeks burn, though, when I look up and see a teenage boy among the soldiers. He holds a hand over his stomach and looks away, ashamed.

When I am down to my underwear, the rowdy soldiers quiet down.

"Where is it then?"

"He's hiding it—off with your pants, boy!" A rusty—and, luckily, dull—bayonet tip swipes at the waistband of my underwear.

"Hey!" I cry, pressing myself back into the crumbly dirt wall.

"That's enough, Edwards. It's clear he's not hiding anything between his legs." The captain gets a round of laughter at that. He stares at me for a long while and then pronounces, "It must be inside the boy."

"Then what are we waiting for?" cries Edwards. "Cut him open!"

"No!" yells the captain, extending his arm to hold back the eager mob. "You kill the boy, and you kill the life source within him."

I nod quickly, finally understanding what Nuru meant when she called me her "host." The captain tosses my clothes back to me, and I quickly dress myself.

"You're more precious to us than gold, boy. What you got inside, it gives us life. See?" He steps closer to me and suddenly his bony arm grows flesh! In a matter of seconds, I see the captain as he once was. Blue eyes fill the empty sockets, and sandy hair sprouts from his no longer bare skull. He makes a fist and pounds it against his chest. "Having you here with us makes me feel like a man again!"

"But...you're dead."

"Ah, yes," he says with a fake regret. Then the captain's frown turns into a fiendish grin. "Dead—but not gone! We have learned to make the most of our...unfortunate condition."

"But why..." I falter and then decide not to ask.

"Yes?"

"Spit it out, boy!" snaps Edwards. "We ain't got all the time in the world to stand here jawin' with you."

I think about asking just what else they have to do, being dead, but decide against it. "Well, why don't you want to return with the other souls? Why stay here...like this?"

The captain only sneers at me. "So you know about the ship, hey? Do you know it'll be packed full of niggers? The fools want to go back to Africa! Now why would civilized men like us want to set sail with a ship full of stinking slaves?"

"I'd rather live in a hole in the ground than set foot on those savage shores," says an older soldier.

"It ain't our home, see?" another explains. "And how do we know what they got in store for us? Maybe they want to turn the tables and make us—free white men—into *their* slaves!"

The captain nods solemnly. "For all we know, your ship may be no better than a British prison hulk—floating death, that's what they call them. I'll keep my feet on solid ground, thank you very much!"

I never imagined ghosts could be racist. I want to ask if they've ever heard of Crispus Attucks or any of the other black men who died fighting in the Revolutionary War. Even though my mother taught me that it's pointless to debate a bigot, I try to reason with the nether beings. "Don't you want to know what peace feels like? The war is over—"

"No it ain't! Not for us. It'll never be over for us," Edwards grumbles bitterly.

"We was ready to surrender but them Hessians—they just kept firing and when they got close enough…" The old soldier drags his finger across his throat.

A younger man picks up the tale. "No mercy did they show our poor boys—no mercy at all. But what can you expect from a pack of foreign mercenaries? They stormed up the hill with their pockets full of blood money."

Finally the teenage boy speaks up. "True—but we held our ground! We didn't turn and run like the rest of those yellow-bellied cowards. We held our ground."

"And we hold it still," says the captain. "Our blood is in this soil." He leans in so close that I can count his blond eyelashes. "We're not going anywhere." To his men he yells, "Restrain the prisoner!"

Nuru was right—the nether beings cannot touch me, but they still manage to weave a cage out of wiry tree roots pulled from the earth. I have barely enough room to take a couple of steps in either direction. In despair, I fall back against the wall and then leap forward to brush the ants and worms off my head and shoulders. How long will I have to stay in this hellish hole? Will the nether beings let me waste away, or will they keep me alive in order to protect the precious being I carry within?

Finally Nuru speaks to me. *D, get close to the ground.*

I'm so relieved to hear her voice that I almost forget not to speak out loud. *Why?*

I need you to send a message, but you must be discreet.

How can I be discreet when all the nether beings want to be close to me? I slide down the wall and pull my knees up to my chest. *OK, I'm ready.*

Use your finger to tap on the ground as loudly as you can. Three beats, followed by a pause, three times. Understand?

The floor is made of dirt. How can I beat the dirt with one finger and hope to make a sound? Who could ever hear such a message? Then I remember Nuru's signal to the dead. It was the vibration that mattered, not the sound. I brush the loose dirt away from the ground near my hand and pick a spot where the earth is packed tight and hard. Using the middle finger of my left hand, I tap out Nuru's message and hope it reaches the right ears.

At first, nothing happens. Then one of the soldiers peers into a tunnel. "Captain," he says, "I think we better send out a scouting party. There's trouble coming, I'm sure of it."

"Take a few men and check it out," says the captain from his lawn chair. He swings his feet up onto the table, unwilling to leave me now that he's able to feel whole once more.

Not wanting to miss out on the action, almost all of the ghost soldiers arm themselves and disappear down the dark tunnel. Only the captain and the teenage boy stay behind. I stand in my root cage trying not to reveal the anxiety I feel inside. I want to be ready to act, but don't know just what is it I should be ready to do.

The boy, who was seated on the floor, suddenly gets to his feet. I try to read the expression on his face, but it's hard—he's too far away from me to have his flesh fully restored. But something tells me he knows what's about to happen. He moves over to the wall and picks up one of the rifles.

"What are you doing, boy?"

"Just cleaning my musket, sir."

The captain mumbles his approval and returns to his book. The boy looks at me as he removes the bayonet from the end of his long gun. He moves closer to my cage, and the flesh blooms on his bones. Now I'm sure of the sympathy in his eyes. "They're coming," he whispers before holding the bayonet blade close to his leg.

Just when I think he's about to pass the blade to me, I see a white spot quivering against the wall beside me. It takes a moment to register, but then I realize someone's pointing a light at me! I scan the cavern, searching for its source, and nearly faint when I see Nyla and Keem crouching by the mouth of one of the tunnels that ring the cavern.

Then everything happens at once. Frantic hollering comes from the tunnel that the scouting party went down, and within seconds mice, rats, and other small furry beasts begin scurrying into the cavern.

"What in damnation?" cries the captain, jumping up and kicking at the frantic creatures that are now spilling into the room. They crawl up the walls, the chairs—even my legs! Then several of the ghost soldiers tumble into the room carried on a virtual wave of feet and fur.

In the chaos, the boy slips his bayonet blade into my cage. I start sawing at the roots from the inside, and he pulls out a hunting knife to hack at them from the outside. Before long we've managed to cut a large enough hole for me to slip through. Now I just have to wade through the sea of vermin in order to reach Nyla and Keem.

13.

I might have slipped away unnoticed if I hadn't been carrying Nuru inside of me. But as soon as I take a step away from the ghost soldiers, the flesh on their bones starts to wither away. At first they're all too busy battling rodents to notice. The captain is stabbing at the poor critters with the bayonet end of his rifle. His back is turned to me, so at first he doesn't notice that I've broken free of the root cage and am heading toward one of the far tunnels. But when the skin on his hands starts to rot, the captain spins around and yells, "You—boy! Get back here!"

When I disobey, the captain barks another command—this time to his troops: "It's a diversion—after him, boys! Don't let him escape!"

I try to run, but I can barely move my feet through the swirling stream of rodents. I fall more than once but keep on inching forward, knowing I'm now being pursued by a mob of ghosts. I keep my eyes glued on the black mouth of the tunnel where I saw Nyla and Keem, but when I finally get there—they're gone.

"Nyla? Keem?" I hear my desperate voice echo down the dark tunnel, but I can't see anyone. Were my eyes playing tricks on me? Did I just imagine my friends had come to rescue me?

Then I hear Nyla's voice up ahead: "Hurry, D—this way!"

I rush forward into the blackness, trailing my hand along the tunnel wall so I don't trip over the steady trickle of mice and rats scampering along the ground. I keep hoping I'll see the white circle of light again, but nothing appears to guide me. Where are they?

Behind me I can hear the curses of the angry ghost soldiers and the tiny shrieks of rodents as they are kicked or stabbed or swept aside. I want to speed up, but I am afraid to plunge further into the darkness alone. I tug at my shirt, hoping to see that light glowing again in my chest, but I can't see, hear, or feel Nuru's presence. I am alone.

Just as my heart sinks in despair, I hear Nyla's voice once more.

"D—up here!"

I turn to face the wall and strain my eyes to see the top of the tunnel. Nyla flicks on her flashlight for just a moment so I can see her face peering out of a small hole. "How'd you get up there?" I ask.

The beam of light wavers as Nyla moves aside to let Keem take her place in the small opening about six feet off the ground. "Never mind—just hurry up!" Keem says.

I reach into the darkness. Keem leans out of the hole, bats my hands aside, and grasps my forearms instead. I hear him grunt as he pulls me up off the ground. I use my feet to climb up the wall, and within a few seconds I'm in the secret tunnel with Nyla and Keem. It is much smaller than the tunnel I just left, and we lie pressed close together as the ghost soldiers pass below us muttering angrily.

"Where's he gone?"

"Bring a torch! Can't find a darkie in the dark."

"We should've skinned him alive while we had the chance!"

"Come on, boys—he don't know these tunnels like we do!"

We feel a rush of icy air, and then there is silence in the tunnel below. Nyla wriggles away from the opening and gestures for us to follow her. We don't say a word until we're deep in the secret tunnel and sure that no one can hear us. The space isn't large enough for any of us to stand, so we sit in a tight circle with Nyla's flashlight in the middle.

"How did you guys find me? And what happened to your arm?"

Nyla touches her right shoulder and then shrugs to prove it's OK. "You tell me, D. One minute blood was oozing from my shoulder, and then you touched me and..."

"And what?"

Keem takes over the story. "By the time I reached her, the bleeding had stopped. I couldn't even tell where the spike went in."

"But—that's impossible!"

"Is it?" asks Nyla. "Earlier today the bird perched on your knee for two seconds, and all of a sudden the wound in your ankle healed up." Nyla watches me as I consider her words—and their implication. "It's inside of you, isn't it—the bird?"

I nod and check for the light in my chest, but there's still no sign of Nuru.

"So that must mean that whatever healing power it had has now passed to you." Nyla takes my hand in hers. "You touched me, remember? I grabbed your hand before you left, and I felt—*something*—shoot up into my arm."

Keem either doesn't notice or doesn't mind that Nyla's still holding my hand. "Can you, like, feel it inside of you?" he asks.

"Not really. But I can still hear her. Nuru's been guiding me...off and on."

"We sure could have used a guide," says Keem. "We followed that stone monster and saw you crawl into the white boulder. But then the creature fell apart and the entrance was covered by a ton of bricks."

Nyla jumps in. "So we started looking for a fallen tree."

"Why?" I ask.

"Remember how we saw the mist coming out of the ground where that old tree had been ripped up by the roots? We figured that must be a way into...their world. But then we found the second boulder, and the plaque on it opened like a door."

"A *small* door," adds Keem.

I almost laugh thinking of long, lean Keem trying to squeeze into an opening not much bigger than a sheet of paper. "So how did you fit through?"

Nyla and Keem look at one another and shrug. "I felt like Alice in Wonderland!" Nyla exclaims. "As soon as I stuck my head in, I either started to shrink or the doorway started to expand."

"Either way, we both got in. It was pitch black in there, but Nyla was prepared."

"I'm no Boy Scout, but I am a military brat." Nyla nods at the compact silver flashlight propped up before us. It's attached to a bundle of keys along with some purple lanyard, a Swiss Army knife, and a small plastic alien that glows green in the dark.

"We went down these stairs that seemed to last forever, and there were two tunnels. Keem thought he heard voices, so we took the tunnel on the left, and that led us straight to you."

Keem nudges me with his massive foot. "Good thing we showed up when we did."

I should say something about how relieved I was to see them, but pride pricks at my throat instead. "Actually, I was just about to break out of there when you guys showed up."

"Yeah, right," scoffs Keem.

"It's true! One of the ghost soldiers helped me escape!"

"Why would a nether being help you?" asks Nyla.

"I don't know—he wasn't like the others. He was young, like us."

You must keep going, D.

I get to my feet. "Come on—Nuru says we have to keep moving."

Nyla and Keem stand—or crouch—and we press forward in silence for a while.

"Where are we going?" asks Nyla. She's in the lead, holding the flashlight.

"I don't know," I confess. "I'm waiting for Nuru to give me directions."

Keem groans. "Ask her if she can find us a bigger tunnel—I can't walk like Quasimodo much longer."

A few moments later, Keem's wish is granted: the small earthen tunnel ends, and we find ourselves in a large cement sewage tunnel. Nyla covers her nose with her hand as she splashes down into the shallow, slimy water. Keem sloshes past her and stretches his limbs. "Free at last!"

"Free?" asks Nyla. "Do either of you know where we are?" She swings the small beam of light around the tunnel, but we barely get a glimpse of our new surroundings before the light flickers and fades. "Crap—the battery's dead. What do we do now?"

Hold out your hand, says Nuru. I do as I'm told and watch in amazement as the warm glow reappears around my heart. It moves up into my shoulder, travels down my arm, and settles in the palm of my hand. I push back against the darkness, and soon we can see clearly enough to move forward again.

The dark, foul-smelling tunnel intersects with others, but we keep going straight ahead. I figure Nuru will let me know if we're heading in the wrong direction. My feet are soaked, and it's colder than when we were in the earthen tunnel under the park. At times we can hear the faint rumble of a nearby subway train, or the ground above will shake as a bus or truck rolls overhead. I don't want to admit it, but I'm glad I'm not alone. The city's alive above us, but no one in that world knows we're down here. If anything happens—if anything *else* happens—we only have each other to rely on. Nuru's inside of me, but she only pipes up when we prove we can't handle the situation ourselves.

Keem and Nyla pick up where they left off, their voices filling the dank, empty space around us.

"Those dead guys sure looked pissed. Who—or what— are the Hessians they were whining about?" asks Keem.

"*Hessen.* They were German soldiers who fought for the British," says Nyla. "Lots of people think they fought for money, but most of them had no choice—they were conscripted."

"Well, those walking corpses back there sure know how to hold a grudge," says Keem.

"It's crazy but...I kind of feel sorry for them," admits Nyla.

"What? Why?" I ask.

"I don't know. It just seems...sad. I can't imagine spending my afterlife being angry all the time."

"Hey—when your number's up, it's up," says Keem. "No point walking the earth terrorizing the living. Save your sympathy for D—he's the one they were trying to cut open!"

"Nyla's right, Keem. The ghost soldiers are bitter because they feel like they were abandoned—left to die while others got away to safety."

"You want us to take you back there so you can help them feel better?" he asks sarcastically.

"No! I'm just saying..."

"This whole scenario reminds me of something," Nyla says. She stops, and for a moment all we can hear is the faint trickling of water somewhere farther down the tunnel. After a moment Nyla haltingly begins:

> Take up our quarrel with the foe:
> To you from failing hands we throw
> The torch; be yours to hold it high.
> If ye break faith with us who die
> We shall not sleep, though poppies grow
> In Flanders fields.

"What's that? Some kind of...prophecy?" I ask.

Nyla shakes her head and sloshes on. "It's a poem. I had to memorize it for Remembrance Day."

"Remembrance Day—what's that?" asks Keem.

"You know—Veteran's Day. It marks the end of World War One." Nyla says the poem over again. "*If ye break faith with us who die, we shall not sleep.* Maybe they feel betrayed. Maybe that's why they aren't at peace."

"So take it out on the Hessians—not us! Talk about a bunch of sore losers."

"War isn't a game, Keem," Nyla says with an edge to her voice.

"What's that supposed to mean?" Keem asks defensively.

"They didn't lose a sports tournament—they lost their lives! Fighting for *this* country."

"So? That's what they signed up for. They weren't drafted, they volunteered."

"And I guess a jock like you would never enlist."

"Why should I? This country's at war with my religion— Uncle Sam doesn't want me joining up. I'm the enemy, remember?"

"The war's on terror—not Islam."

"Oh yeah? Too bad most Americans don't know the difference!"

Finally I spin around and hold up my hand so that the bright light stuns them both into silence. "All right, you guys—that's enough!" Suddenly I hear something whimpering behind us. I know the sound didn't come from Nyla or Keem—they're heated, not sad or scared.

"What was that?" I ask.

"What was what?" Keem looks around warily.

"Shhh—listen."

We freeze and strain our ears to hear the strange sound that caught my attention.

"It's coming from over there," whispers Nyla, pointing to a corner where two sewage tunnels intersect.

I slowly walk over to the dark corner. Something white is cowering near the ground. When the white bones disappear as I approach, I know it's one of the dead. I tell Nyla and Keem to stay back. As I get closer, the crouching skeleton takes on flesh and becomes a crouching boy.

"Are you OK?" I ask.

"The light…" he says in a hoarse voice, his hand shielding his eyes.

I pull my sleeve down over my hand to dim the light generated by Nuru. "Is that better?"

He nods and slowly pushes himself up the curved wall of the tunnel.

"It's you! You helped me escape." The boy nods and tries to smile, but it seems he's forgotten how to look—or feel—happy. "Thanks," I say. "I owe you one."

"You OK, D?" Keem's deep voice booms down the tunnel, frightening the boy.

"It's OK," I assure him. "My friends are with me." I call over my shoulder, "It's the boy who helped me." This time the boy forms a genuine smile. "What's your name?" I ask.

"Billy," he says, standing up straight.

"Is it all right if my friends come and meet you?"

Billy gives a nervous nod and tries to make himself more presentable. He runs a hand through his stringy hair and then pulls his jacket closed to hide the bayonet wound that tore open his stomach more than two hundred years ago.

I motion for Nyla and Keem to join us. They aren't too sure how to greet a ghost, so they just nod and say, "Hey." It's clear that Keem doesn't trust Billy at all, but I do.

"So…you followed us?" I ask.

Billy nods and clears his throat. "I—I just wanted to ask…that is, I hoped you might…"

"Yes?"

"Could I—could I come with you?"

Before I can answer, he rushes on. "I won't be no trouble, I swear I won't. I just…I don't want to live like this no more. We can't eat, we can't sleep—we can't do nothing like we used to when we was alive. I'd give anything just to be able to shake your hand!" Billy hangs his head. "I didn't know it would be like this when I joined up. When the end came, I was so angry—it wasn't fair! This wasn't supposed to happen to me. I'm just a boy…"

Keem grunts with contempt. "You *were* a soldier—now you're a ghost. How do we know you're not also a spy?"

"Keem!" Nyla steps in front of him and smiles at Billy. "Ignore him, Billy. Of course you can come with us."

Determined to be heard, Keem steps around Nyla. "You're not calling the shots, Nyla. This ghost isn't one of us—he's one of them! Have you forgotten everything they put us through?"

"I didn't want to hurt you, I swear!" Billy protests. "I was just following orders…"

"Famous last words," mutters Keem.

Nyla's anger flares again. "You don't know what it takes to break ranks like that. If a soldier did that today, he'd face a court martial."

"He's DEAD, Nyla!"

"Whatever…"

I see the panic in Billy's eyes and know I can't turn him away. "He did help me, Keem—without being asked. I don't think Billy's loyal to the nether beings—not anymore. Besides, he's harmless now. The ghost soldiers lose their power once they leave the park." I turn to Billy for confirmation. "Right?"

"Well…sort of."

"Sort of?" Keem repeats Billy's words with suspicion.

"Mostly. We're strongest in the park because that's where—I mean, that's where it all happened."

"Where you died," says Nyla.

"Right. But when we leave the park…"

"Yes?" I need Billy to tell us everything even though I'm pretty sure his news won't be good.

"Our spirits can join with others who are…like us. We draw on their energy—their rage."

"Great—a club for pissed-off dead folks," says Keem.

"The murder rate in New York City's no joke," says Nyla. "There must be dead people all over the place."

Billy nods somberly. "There's a lot of misery in this land."

"Why did you help me?" I ask.

Billy hangs his head so that strands of his brown hair fall forward and cover his eyes. "I had a friend like you once," he admits, nodding in my direction.

"You mean—he was black?"

Billy lifts up his chin. "Color don't bother me none. Jake was every bit as brave as me—he'd have fought alongside the rest of us if his master had let him."

"He was a slave?" asks Nyla.

"Yes. He was born a slave, and for all I know, he died a slave. And there we were fighting for *liberty*." Billy's lips twist with bitterness. "Ma said it was right to fight the British. She come over on a ship as a girl, and it took seven years to work off her indenture. But at the end of it, she was free. Jake and his mama—they weren't ever going to get that chance." Billy pauses and then looks up at me. "You think I'll see my mother and Jake up in heaven?"

Nyla and Keem join Billy in staring at me. I try not to squirm before their expectation that I ought to know where the ship of souls is heading. When I asked Nuru if I would see my mother again, she said the ship was only for those who were "long dead." Does that include Billy's mother? Finally I say, "I don't know, Billy. Nuru said the souls of the dead are seeking peace, and so she's going to take them back to her realm."

"Is that Africa?" Billy asks.

I shrug and hope I won't have to answer any more questions. "We better get going. What time is it?"

Keem checks the lit display on his watch. "Just past one a.m. No wonder I'm beat."

"I'm starving, too," admits Nyla. "Can we rest for a little while?"

"You all can rest—I'll keep watch," offers Billy.

"Hmph. I know I'll be sleeping with one eye open," Keem mutters as he looks around for a dry section of the tunnel.

"Shut up already," Nyla snaps irritably.

Keem takes the bag of chips out of his book bag and tosses it at Nyla. "I hope you don't talk in your sleep 'cause I sure am tired of hearing your mouth."

"We'll never get any rest if you two keep fighting," I say. "We're a team, remember?"

Grumbling under their breath, Keem and Nyla move off in opposite directions. Billy watches them go, then turns and reverts to his skeleton self as he heads away from me and back up the way we've come. I decide to stay close to Nyla—partly because I'm hungry, too, and she's got the chips. I think about what Billy told us—how other people's rage fuels the nether beings—and wonder if it's affecting Nyla and Keem, too.

I push my sleeve back up and find that the light in my hand has dimmed. Maybe Nuru's tired as well. I clear my throat and try to find out what's up with Nyla. "Keem's not such a bad guy, you know."

Nyla says nothing. We're in a narrow tunnel that only has a thin stream of water running down its center. Nyla slides down the tunnel wall until she's crouched on the dry part. She sticks out her foot and pins a bloated plastic bag that's slowly floating by on the slimy water. "What are you—his cheerleader?"

"No! I just wondered what happened to change your mind about him. You two seemed pretty tight before."

Nyla sighs. She doesn't seem to have the strength to act fierce anymore. "It's always that way with guys. Things start out fine and then…"

"Then what?"

She shrugs. "Things change—that's what."

"Maybe you just haven't met the right guy yet," I say hopefully.

Nyla gives a tired laugh. "Maybe." She shakes her foot and sets the bag free. We both watch as it floats away. "Maybe there is no Mr. Right. Not for me."

I really don't know what to say to that, so I ask for some chips instead. We eat in silence for a while, and then I suggest that we try to get some rest. Nyla tips her head back against the hard tunnel wall and closes her eyes, ending our conversation. I drift off, too, and wake a few hours later when I feel a strange fluttering inside my chest. *Wake up, D. We must proceed across the river. The ship awaits.*

I shake Nyla gently until she wakes up. Then I go looking for Keem. He's stretched out in a short, dry tunnel that's filled with the soft light of dawn. In the distance, through a rusty grate, I can see the Statue of Liberty out in the river. We've come a long way from the park. We outran the nether beings and we're close to fulfilling Nuru's mission. I have to admit, I feel pretty proud of myself—and my friends. Then my good feeling disappears and I think about how much I'll miss the city—and Nyla and Keem—when I'm gone.

Keem mumbles something in his sleep, and I remember Nuru's message. "Wake up, Keem. We've got to keep going."

To my surprise, Keem sits up and looks completely alert. "Give me a few minutes," he says in a gruff voice.

"For what?" I ask, but before Keem can answer, Nyla calls me over to her.

"Give him some privacy," she says. "He probably wants to pray."

I follow Nyla away from the mouth of the tunnel but glance back over my shoulder and see Keem on his knees. He takes up some of the dust on the floor of the dry tunnel and rubs it over his hands and forearms. I want to keep watching but decide I'd better find my own private corner and handle my business. After I'm done I say a quick prayer of my own.

A few minutes later, we gather in the main sewage tunnel and try to decide on the best way to cross the river. Nuru's light burns bright in the palm of my hand, but I make a fist to shield Billy from the glare.

"So where is this ship docked?" Nyla asks.

"Docked?"

"Are we heading to a pier or something?" asks Keem.

I look at him and take a deep breath. "The ship is with the dead," I explain.

Keem frowns. "And where are the dead?"

"Underground?" I don't mean it to come out like a question, but I'm not really sure that's the right answer. Nuru doesn't correct me, though.

Keem rolls his eyes as if to say, "Of course." Then he lays out his plan. "I say we find a way out of here, take the train into the city, and then find another way underground once we get there."

"We can't do that," I say.

"Why not?" asks Nyla.

"Billy can't go outside the way we can. We'd have to wait until dark, and even then he couldn't ride the train with us."

"Maybe he could stay underground and meet us there," Nyla suggests.

I shake my head. "He doesn't know the way. Only Nuru does." An awkward silence settles between us. "Look, you guys—I couldn't have made it this far without you, but maybe it's time for you to go back."

"You're ditching us for that ghost?" Keem asks, indignant.

"We have to stay down here—you don't. Maybe we can find a manhole or something and you can go back to the real world."

"I'm not leaving you down here by yourself, D," Nyla says, determined.

"I'm not alone—I have Nuru and Billy."

"Well, I'm not going anywhere with him." Nyla nods in Keem's direction and folds her arms across her chest.

I'm not sure what to say to that, but there's no time to think because Billy pipes up all of a sudden. "We should hurry," he says in an anxious voice.

"Why? What's the rush?" asks Keem.

"We should go—*now*," Billy says, ignoring Keem and looking straight at me.

"What's wrong, Billy?" asks Nyla.

"I can feel them," he replies with a shudder. "They're coming for me."

14.

"*TRAITOR!*"

All of us freeze as the hissing voices echo down the dark tunnel.

Billy turns to me, a look of terror on his pale face. "Go—run!"

"You're coming with us," I say. "We'll find a way to get across the river—you'll be safe with us."

"No—I'll only slow you down. Get above ground—get into the light. They can't follow you up there."

Nyla tugs at my arm. "He's right, D—let's go."

"There's some kind of ladder over there," says Keem. "It must lead up to a manhole or grate."

I don't look to see where Keem's pointing. I look into Billy's eyes and see the pain that time hasn't healed. He wasn't much older than me when he went off to war and died a horrible death while his fellow soldiers fled to safety. "I'm not leaving you, Billy."

"D—"

I stop Nyla before she can try to change my mind. "You two take the ladder. Come on, Billy—we can outrun them."

Billy steps away from my outstretched arm. "No, we can't—they'll just follow us until they wear us down. But I can distract them—I'll lead them away from you!"

"What will they do once they find you?" asks Nyla.

Billy shrugs, but it's clear he's terrified. "What *can* they do? I'm already dead."

"Listen," I say, and we all grow silent as a soft rumbling moves the water at our feet.

"It's a train," says Keem.

"It's *our* train," I tell him, getting ready to break into a run. "Don't give up, Billy. We can win this battle—just trust me!"

With one last glance over his shoulder, Billy nods at me and together we race down the tunnel in search of the oncoming train. We don't stop until we come to a sort of intersection. Our tunnel ends and we have to jump down into a knee-deep pool of water. I look up and am surprised to see an arched brick ceiling overhead. If I didn't know we were in a sewer, I'd think we were in an old church or even a castle. Then a heap of trash on a wide ledge above us catches my eye. I see stacks of plaid shopping bags stuffed to their limit, and two metal grocery carts brimming with equally full plastic bags. Who could have brought so much stuff down here?

Keem nudges me. "Which way?"

I'm about to say, "I don't know," when a woman's voice booms in the cavernous space.

"HEY!"

I jump and grab hold of Nyla's arm. She doesn't look scared, but I can feel how tense her arm is.

"Who's there?" Nyla asks in a defiant voice.

We all scan the damp, dim space, knowing we have to be ready to fight or flee. Billy silently points to a white candle burning on the far ledge. The flame flickers as the pile of trash starts moving—and then talks to us!

"What you kids doin' down here? This ain't for you—this is my world, *my* world!"

The angry voice belongs to a woman—at least it sounds like a woman. She's wearing a wool cap and square black sunglasses like the ones Mrs. Martin wears for her cataracts.

"Is that a—bag lady?" Keem keeps his voice down, but the woman still hears him and takes offense.

"I heard that!" she cries, standing up. "You think you can come down here and disrespect me? I'll show you. I'll teach you to show respect." Agitated, the woman starts rifling through her heap of bags.

I've seen homeless people before, and I know that some of them band together, forming communities in hidden corners of the city. But I never expected to meet a homeless woman down here. I want to ask how she eats and bathes and lives without light—is she really down here alone? But then I decide I better try to do some damage control instead, otherwise we may end up fighting ghost soldiers *and* an army of homeless people. I step forward and let my home training lead the way. "Uh—we're sorry to bother you…ma'am. We're just trying to find the train."

The woman stops rummaging through her bags and glares at me. "Train? This look like Grand Central Station to you?"

"No, ma'am, but—well…"

Nyla gives an exasperated sigh. "We're in trouble—can you help us?"

The woman adjusts her sunglasses and sniffs the air. Is she blind? Why else would she wear dark glasses in such a dark place?

"Trouble? What kind of trouble?" she asks angrily.

I look at my friends, hoping they'll have an answer that will make sense to this strange woman. Before any of us can say anything, she starts mumbling to herself again and roots through one of the jam-packed grocery carts.

"Kids always bring trouble, that's all they do. Up there they always be messin' with me when I ain't done nothin' to bother them. I mind my own business, I keep to myself." She stops muttering, pulls a golf club out of her cart, and shouts at us, "I don't want no trouble! Why you think I moved down here? All I ever wanted was to be left alone…"

"I'm sorry—we don't mean to disturb you. But…" I pause and search for words to explain our dilemma. "Something's after us—something evil. We have to get away!"

"Ain't nothin' down here but rats. And they won't bother you if you don't bother them."

An eerie, anguished moan drifts down the dark tunnel. The woman freezes and peers into the blackness. She looks alert but unafraid. "Trouble comin' for sure," she mutters, taking a few practice swings with her golf club. Then she looks at us hard, her gaze settling on Billy's pale face. "Where you tryin' to go?"

"Into the city—we need to take the train," I say.

"I seen fools die tryin' to surf them trains. You aimin' to die young?"

"No, ma'am. We're trying to stay alive. But—" I glance over my shoulder. "We have to go—now!"

She stares at us for another long moment, then turns and points to a small square opening above one of the brick ledges. "Pull off that grate. You gonna have to crawl on your belly 'cause it's tight in there. When you come out the other end, you'll see the tracks. Stay away from that third rail or you'll fry—you hear me?"

"Yes, ma'am. And thank you—thank you!"

She waves me off and starts pulling the grocery carts around her to form a protective wall. I want to say something more—warn her about what's coming, but there's no time. I turn around and see that Keem has already pulled the grate off the wall. He stoops a bit and makes a step for Nyla by locking his fingers together. Nyla accepts the boost without a word of thanks and pulls herself into the square air vent. Keem hoists me up next, then jumps up and pulls himself into the vent without any help.

I use my knees and forearms to pull myself forward, then stop. "Where's Billy?"

"He's behind me—hurry up, D!" Keem gives my foot a shove and I wriggle faster. When I reach the end, Nyla reaches up her hands to pull me out of the vent. We both pull Keem out, and Billy manages on his own.

"Watch out for the third rail," warns Keem, pointing to the hooded rail running along the far side of the tracks. "Try to stay in the middle."

We do our best to follow Keem's instructions, stumbling over trash and splashing through puddles as we move forward. Up ahead we can see white lights shining above the station platform.

"Wait a minute," Nyla says, holding up her hand. We all stop and listen as a distant roar rumbles behind us.

"TRAIN!" shouts Keem, pulling me into a shallow alcove along the tunnel wall. Nyla and Billy do the same, and we all cover our ears as the silver train streaks by.

"Come on—run!" yells Nyla.

We step back into the tracks and race after the train, which is slowing down to pick up passengers at the station up ahead. Keem reaches the train first and easily pulls himself up onto the back of the last car. He reaches down and pulls Nyla up beside him, then they both do the same for me.

I turn and hold out my hand to pull Billy up, but he's retreating back down the tunnel. "Billy!" I try to jump back down onto the tracks, but Keem and Nyla hold me back. "Billy—don't go! Don't give up!"

The flesh on Billy's bones disintegrates as he moves farther away from me. "The light…"

"You can do it, Billy—don't be afraid!"

Billy stops retreating but stands in the middle of the tracks shaking his head. "I can't. I can't…"

"Leave him, D." Keem wraps his strong arm across my chest as the familiar *ding-dong* signals that the doors of the train are closing. In another couple of seconds, the train will pull out of the station.

"Billy, *please*!" I lean forward as far as I can and hold out my hand.

Billy turns, and whatever he sees in the darkness of the tunnel propels him forward into the light. The train heaves and surges ahead. Billy breaks into a run. Nyla gasps and points at the angry fingers of gray mist licking at Billy's heels.

"Traitor!"

"Hurry, Billy," I cry out. "Take my hand. TAKE MY HAND!"

Billy runs harder, flinching as the bright lights from the subway platform beat down on him. The flesh returns to his bones as Billy catches up to the train. My heart pounds in my chest as I will Billy not to fall, not to stop, not to give up. Then Billy looks up into my eyes, and in a split second I see his fear vanish. He makes a desperate leap, and a crackling flash of light blinds us all as Billy's fingers grab hold of mine. I pull him up onto the narrow ledge and proudly shout, "You did it, Billy—you did it!"

I don't know if anyone can hear me above the deafening groans of the train. The four of us huddle close together. We hold on for dear life as the train hurtles through the darkness and carries us under the river and into lower Manhattan.

When the train finally slows and pulls into the next station, Nuru speaks to me. I hop down onto the tracks, and the others follow me without question. We walk back down the tracks until we come to a metal door that's been painted bright yellow. A sign on the door says, "Authorized personnel only." But Nuru says, *Proceed*, so I try the doorknob and find that it isn't locked. A short hallway lit by a caged bulb leads us into another train tunnel. There are tracks on the ground, but the tunnel doesn't seem like it has been used in a long time. Instead of soot-covered concrete, the curved walls are made of reddish-brown bricks. The air is warm, and there isn't any water trickling down the walls or pooling between the rails.

We are nearly there, D. Hold out your hand.

I do as I'm told and lift my arm up so that Nuru's light will guide us through the darkness. "Nuru says we're almost there."

Nyla and Keem nod silently to let me know they're ready to go on. I turn to Billy and see that he's trembling. "Billy—are you OK?"

He stares at his hands and then points at me. "You… you…"

I put my hand on his shoulder and try my best to reassure him. "It's all right, Billy—we're safe. The nether beings can't reach us now."

Billy shakes his head but not because he doesn't believe me. "You…*touched* me," he says softly. Billy looks at me with tear-filled eyes and then stares down at his hands once more. Tears fall into his palms as he holds them out, transfixed. For the first time, I notice that the gray gloom has left his body. Billy glows with light that is pale, but warm. "I…I can *feel* again," he says, amazed.

Keem steps up and holds out his hand. "We couldn't do this before."

Billy stares at Keem's hand for several seconds, then reaches out and shakes it heartily. Billy's excitement spreads, and we all start to laugh as Keem tries to teach him the homeboy handshake. Billy turns to Nyla next, but she doesn't hold out her hand—Nyla opens her arms and folds Billy inside. Our laughter dies when we realize that Billy's sobbing. Nyla doesn't let go. Keem turns away and clears his throat. I wipe away my own tears with the back of my sleeve. It's been three months since my mother wrapped me in her arms. I can't even imagine waiting more than two hundred years for someone else to hug me. For just a moment, I think of Mrs. Martin and how it was between us before Mercy arrived. Nuru's voice helps me push those thoughts aside.

We must not delay. Follow this tunnel to the Chamber of Souls.

"We're almost there," I tell my companions. Then I take a deep breath, banish all thoughts of the past, and say, "Let's do this."

There's an eerie silence in this new tunnel. No sound penetrates the curved brick walls, and with each step forward, I feel as if I'm leaving reality behind. A moment ago we clung to a sleek, silver train—now we seem to be sliding into the past, leaving technology behind.

"That's weird—my watch stopped. Anybody got the time?" asks Keem.

Billy and I shake our heads. Keem opens his mouth to say something else but sighs heavily instead. Nuru's light burns bright above, but we all slow down as a heavy, invisible burden settles upon us.

Suddenly Nyla gasps and clamps a hand over her mouth. Tears squeeze out of her closed eyes and trickle down her cheek. Keem reaches her before I do. Without a word he slips his arm around her shoulder and helps her to keep moving forward.

Billy frowns and looks at me. "Do you feel it, too?"

I nod and look around the still, silent tunnel. "It's like wading through a sea of grief."

"What could have caused so much suffering?" asks Billy.

"We're not far from Ground Zero," Keem says quietly.

Nyla clears her throat and wipes her eyes. "Can you help these souls, D? They deserve to be at peace, too."

"I don't know," I answer truthfully. "I hope so." I glance back and see that Keem has removed his arm from Nyla's shoulder. They're holding hands instead.

We walk in silence for a long time. The sad feeling in the tunnel doesn't disappear, but the hope in our hearts gives us the strength to go on. Then Billy points at something up ahead. "Look—we've reached the end."

A brick wall chokes off the tunnel and stops us in our tracks. I shine Nuru's light over the wall and notice that the rails don't end—they seem to run right under the wall.

"They must have sealed off this old tunnel back when the trains went electric," says Keem. "There's no third rail down here."

"These bricks do look old," adds Nyla, running her fingers over the wall's façade.

Nuru, I say in my mind. *What do we do now?*

But all Nuru says is, *Proceed.*

"We have to find a way to break through," I tell my companions. "Any ideas?"

"Anybody got a sledgehammer?" asks Keem sarcastically.

"We might not need one," says Nyla. "The mortar around these bricks is crumbling—some of them are already loose."

We all join Nyla and run our hands over the bricks, looking for signs of decay. I'm the shortest, so I try the ones closest to the ground. I find one brick that already has a chipped corner. I pull my keys from my pocket and dig at the surrounding mortar until I can grab hold of the brick with my fingers. "I've got one!" I cry.

Since I've only got one free hand, I step back and hold the light up high while the others finish the job. Nyla uses her fingernails to get a grip on the loose brick and then jiggles it back and forth until it starts to slide out of place. "You're going to owe me a manicure, D," she says with a smile. "There—I did it!"

Nyla pulls the brick out of the wall and holds it up to show the rest of us. Billy takes it from her, and Keem kneels down beside her to see if he can loosen the surrounding bricks. Before long they've managed to pull out a dozen more, leaving a hole in the wall that's big enough to crawl through.

"After you," says Keem with a dramatic sweep of his arm.

I get down on my knees and stick my hand through first so I can see what lies ahead. Nuru's light doesn't reveal much, though, and the only thing I notice is the silky softness of the dirt on the ground. I crawl through the opening we made in the brick wall and find that the train tracks don't extend beyond the barrier. I hold my hand high above my head but can't find any walls other than the one at my back. Nuru says nothing but I'm pretty sure we've reached the Chamber of Souls.

Billy crawls through the opening next, followed by Nyla and Keem. I don't have to tell them that we've entered another world—the world of the dead. Before we can take one step forward, a wave of sound rolls toward us, building in volume and intensity. With nowhere to run, we let the wave press us back against the brick wall. It's the scariest sound I've ever heard—hundreds of souls groaning in agony!

Nyla grabs hold of my arm. "Is that...the dead?"

"I guess so," I say, hoping I don't look as scared as I feel.

"They don't sound too happy to see you," Keem says nervously.

I try to keep the fear out of my voice. "It's Nuru they've been waiting for all this time, not me."

"They're just restless," says Billy, giving my shoulder a reassuring squeeze. "They know the end is near."

When the wave of sound ebbs into the darkness, I push myself away from the wall and plunge forward with my hand held high. Nyla, Keem, and Billy follow my lead. Our feet make no sound on the feathery dust. We stay close together and try not to lose our bearings in the vast open space. Nuru's light burns bright in my raised hand, but so far there is nothing to see. Then another sound sails toward us on soft currents of black air. This time we rush toward the sound instead of falling back.

Have you ever seen a living hymn—music so vibrant that it shapes the air? Praise songs light the gloom, turning the void into a moonlit beach. Voices swirl around us like stars, and words of rapture dance about our heads like beautiful moths drawn to Nuru's unfailing light. We hear bells, sighs, cries of hallelujah! There are songs of joy sung in a hundred different languages, yet somehow we understand everything.

And then we see them—the dead! They stand in rows, heads bowed, arms folded across their chests like mummies from ancient Egypt. They are skeletons—bleached bones glow like polished ivory in the dark—but they sway with the grace of fifteen thousand dancers. As we draw closer, we see among their bones strands of blue beads, gold buttons, cowrie shells, and coins—all the reminders of home that have endured over the centuries.

I look down upon the dead and feel myself thinning, expanding, blossoming like a flower. I see Nuru's light pouring down from my raised hand, and then I blink and no longer sense my hand, my arm, or my body—I am filled with light. I *am* the light.

Somewhere below and behind me I can hear Nyla's faint voice calling my name, but I feel no urge to respond or turn back. Billy stands with the dead, tears streaming down his face. And then Nuru speaks through me in a voice that rings like a gong: *Awake, my beloved! It is time.*

And with that, the light that I am shoots up into the air and explodes in brilliant sparks like the final firecracker on the Fourth of July. I feel the fluttering of wings as parts of me drift down upon the dead, settling upon the stark white bones *as flesh.* I am a magnificent star shining overhead, and below me are the dead awakened, hands clasped, arms raised in victory.

Then the ship arrives on serene black waves. The dead stop rejoicing and stand in silent awe as the vessel drifts in from afar. I smell salt in the dark air. The dead say a prayer of thanks and then form a solemn procession heading toward the ship's gangplank. I watch the newly embodied souls helping one another, shepherding children on board. Very few among the dead are aged. Most died too soon, their lives cut short by the hardships of slavery. Billy moves among them, lifting infants up so they can be folded into the waiting arms of those already on deck. He beams with purpose and moves with the certainty of one who has found his place. He is white, yet he belongs. This journey will not be like the hellish crossing of those souls stolen from Africa so long ago.

A gust of sea wind fills the sails, and the wooden beams creak as the loaded ship rises on swelling waves. From above I see myself standing beside Billy on the deck. From below I see myself as a shining star high in the night sky. Then, as the ship pulls away from the shore, the sky turns pink and peach as the star becomes the sun. The dawn fills me with warmth and radiant light. I float in a cloudless blue sky as squawking gulls accompany us out to sea.

I see myself standing upon the deck, basking in the sun. I see the sun shining above me. I am both. I am complete. I am content.

Then I hear Nuru's voice.

Look into your heart, D, and tell me what you see.

"Light!" I exclaim ecstatically. "Everywhere there is light."

Look again, my child. Do you really wish to leave this world behind?

"Yes!" I cry without hesitation. "You said it yourself, I have nothing to lose. I want to see your realm."

Won't you miss your friends?

Suddenly I hear Nyla weeping softly. I don't need to turn around to know that she is standing on the shore, wrapped tightly in Keem's strong arms. Though he makes no sound, I can see the tears shining on Keem's cheeks as well. "They have each other," I say without a trace of envy or regret. "They don't need me. You told me once that everyone belonged somewhere. I belong with you. Right?"

You have been an excellent host, D. But—

"But what?" I see a cloud manifest in the azure sky. It threatens to pass before the sun. "You said we had to stay together from now on. You said you'd never let go!"

Even if I release you from service, I will always be with you, D.

"'Release me?' You can't—you can't do that!" My voice gets louder as the ominous cloud creeps across the sun, dimming its glorious light. I can feel a storm of hysteria swirling within me. "I thought you were different. Everyone leaves me behind—everyone!"

You are my host, D. Through you, a part of me can continue to live in this world.

A sob slips from my throat. "I don't have anyone to go back to."

You have two loyal friends. And your foster mother is missing you now—she cares about you, D.

"No she doesn't! Mrs. Martin only cares about Perfect-me. She doesn't even know who I am."

You haven't given her a chance. I knew you were special because you opened your heart to me. If you are honest with others, they too will see your worth.

Billy holds me close and whispers, "Farewell, friend."

I turn to the sun. The sun turns to me.

It is time, D. I must return to my realm. And you must return to yours.

"Please...don't leave me. Don't go!" I cry helplessly.

Hold fast to my love, D. Let it be the light that guides you home.

Another cloud passes in front of the sun. I search the ship deck but can no longer see myself there among the dead. Then there is total darkness as the rolling waves embrace me and pull me back to shore.

15.

I wake to the sound of water splashing below. Under my hands I feel the cold metal of the railing on Lullwater Bridge. I stare down into the lake and in its depths see a small ship trailing a brilliant star. "Good-bye, Nuru," I whisper.

I am not gone, D, she answers. *You will find me when you look within.*

I smile and gaze at the sinking star until it disappears from sight. Then I look up and see Nyla and Keem holding hands by the boathouse. I cross the bridge and join my friends on the far side of the lake.

"Missed me, huh?"

I roll my eyes at Keem but can't keep myself from grinning.

Nyla drops his hand and pulls me into her arms. "Welcome back, freak," she whispers in my ear.

My hand automatically reaches for the sharp pin inside my coat pocket, but then I realize that I don't need to draw blood to truly feel what's in my heart. I hold onto Nyla instead and bury my face in her neck as hot tears spill from my eyes.

I feel Keem's big hand resting gently on the back of my head. "We got you, D," he says quietly. "We got you."

THE END

ACKNOWLEDGMENTS

I'm blessed to have many friends who believe in magic, and as many family members who believe in miracles.

I thank my friend, Gabrielle, who listened to my summary of the story in its early stages and insisted that I let D live. Stefanie helped me work out the plot as we jogged around Prospect Park; Kate read the earliest draft and assured me that the story was complex and compelling. My writer friends on Facebook cheered each time I posted my word count over the holidays. Belonging to a community of artists is invaluable, and I thank all those who respect my need for solitude and welcome me back when the writing's done—especially Rosa, who calls even when she knows I won't pick up. I thank my book blogger friends for keeping me in the loop and for being steadfast supporters of my work.

Marvin Broome and Annemarie Shrouder taught me how to curse in German; my student, Naa Addico, enlisted her grandmother's assistance when I needed help with West African languages. I appreciate their help, but I am responsible for any translation errors.

The park rangers at the African Burial Ground National Monument are phenomenal—informed, impassioned, and always willing to help. I thank Lead Park Ranger Douglas

Massenburg for introducing me to Dr. Muhammad Hatim of the Imams Council of New York. Dr. Muhammad and Umar Al-Uqdah taught me about their faith, and I'm extremely grateful for their generosity.

Prospect Park is a vast wonderland in the heart of Brooklyn. I have wandered its paths since first moving to the city in 1994, and the park continues to soothe and inspire me. I thank the Prospect Park Alliance for preserving its beauty and history.

I want to thank my agent, Faith Childs, who read the manuscript and responded with enthusiasm and encouragement. I also thank her for persisting in an industry where doors and minds are so often closed to writers like me.

Lastly I thank the AmazonEncore team for keeping their door open.

ABOUT THE AUTHOR

Born in Canada, Zetta Elliott moved to Brooklyn in 1994 to pursue her PhD in American studies at New York University. Her poetry and essays have been published in several anthologies, and her plays have been staged in New York, Chicago, and Cleveland. She wrote the award-winning picture book *Bird* and the young adult novel *A Wish After Midnight*. She currently lives in Brooklyn.

Ship of Souls
Discussion Topics and Writing Activities

1. The novel begins with D overhearing a conversation between his mother and a stranger he thinks is his father. Why do you think D's mother wouldn't let the man inside? Pretend that you are D's father and write a letter to your son explaining why you've been absent for so long.

2. Cemeteries are considered "sacred ground," yet the African Burial Ground was nearly destroyed by construction in lower Manhattan. Visit the site (or the Web site: http://www.nps.gov/afbg/index.htm) and learn what life was like for the enslaved men, women, and children who were buried there. What jobs did they perform? What clues were found during the archaeological dig that prove these people still felt connected to Africa?

3. What important historical sites can be found in your community? Choose one site and write a magical scene that might unfold there late at night.

4. Many historical sites don't have a plaque or monument to explain their significance. Design a marker, sculp-

ture, or sign to pay tribute to an important person, place, or event from your community's past.

5. Enslaved Africans built the wall that ran along Wall Street, and they widened the Lenape Trail that became Broadway. When did slavery end in New York State? Learn more about the history of slavery where you live. What contributions did enslaved people make in your state?

6. Some blacks fought alongside the Americans in the Revolutionary War, and others sided with the British who promised them their freedom. Pretend that you are Jake, Billy's enslaved friend. Write a monologue in which Jake explains why he wants to fight in the war. Which side would Jake choose?

7. Keem is a popular school athlete, yet he still gets teased because of his religion. Keem tells D that everyone has to fight for respect. How do you earn the respect of others?

8. Nyla calls D a "freak." Is that an insult or a compliment? What is "the freak's Golden Rule"? Write five rules that you expect your friends to follow.

9. Nuru never explains how she escaped from the nether beings, though she admits that she had help from "burrowing creatures." Write a scene that explains how Nuru managed to become free.

10. Nyla resents the way she's treated by guys on the street, yet Keem says some girls enjoy that kind of attention. What kind of behavior do you find offensive, and what do you do when someone disrespects you? Write a "survival guide" for teenage girls or boys to help them avoid and/or address sexual harassment.

11. Forty percent of the remains found in the African Burial Ground belonged to children. Imagine that D met one of those children in the Chamber of Souls. What kind of conversation do you think they would have? Write a short play in which D, Keem, Nyla, or Billy talks with an enslaved child about his or her life. What might they have in common? What are the advantages of being a child in the twenty-first century?